The Ghost
of
Northumberland
Strait

Lori Knutson

Napoleon

Cover art and design by Vasiliki Lenis

We acknowledge the support of the Canada Council for the Arts for our publishing program. We acknowledge the financial support of the Government of Canada through the Book Publishing Industry Development Program (BPIDP) for our publishing activities.

Napoleon Publishing
an imprint of Napoleon & Company
Toronto, Ontario, Canada
www.napoleonandcompany.com

Printed in Canada

12 11 10 09 08   5 4 3 2 1

Library and Archives Canada Cataloguing in Publication

Knutson, Lori
        The ghost of Northumberland Strait / Lori Knutson.

ISBN 978-1-894917-43-8

        I. Title.
PS8621.N88G46 2008   jC813'.6   C2008-900096-X

For the Sabine Family
of O'Leary, PEI,
with gratitude

One

It's so creepy in this old house. Am I the only one who feels it, or do Nikki and her newest, stupidest boyfriend Mark sense that something's up, too? Derek seems as on edge as me, but does he think anything's wrong? Does he feel that someone's home and watching us break into their house, their eyes on us constantly? Seeing us treat their stuff badly?

I'll tell you, I've had my house broken into, and I sure didn't appreciate it. That was back in Alberta, a few years ago.

We were getting back from a long drive, the whole family. We'd been visiting Aunt Kathy and Uncle Richard over spring break, way up north in Spirit River. Nikki can always sleep in the car. Wish I could. Most of the way home, she sat there, head back, mouth open, snoring like a chainsaw. As soon as I'd start to fall asleep, I'd feel sick to my stomach.

When Dad pulled into our steep driveway, I was so relieved to finally be home. That was just way too much time to be trapped in a moving vehicle with my parents and a snoring sister. It was dark out, but as soon as the headlights hit the garage door, we all saw the damage. Dad said something I shouldn't repeat, and Mom said, "Darwin! The kids!" As if it was something I'd never heard before. Mom looked back over her shoulder at me to see if I'd burst into flame at hearing Dad swear. I just played dumb and pretended not to have heard. It made Mom feel better.

The three of us hopped out as Nikki began to regain consciousness, and as soon as she understood what was going on, she was up and out of the car, too. The garage door was pried open from the bottom like a tin can. It was dented, and a lot of the paint was scraped away. The thieves had stolen most of Dad's tools. As he said, "Anything worth anything" was gone.

They weren't only thieves; they were vandals. Mom had planned to refinish the patio furniture later on that spring and had bought four cans of blue spray paint. There were blue streaks up and down the walls, on the concrete floor, and on the inside of the garage door. The vandals had also painted the inside of the garage window so that no light could get in. The empty cans were scattered on the floor. That mess was bad enough. Then I saw my bike.

I'd gotten the bike at Christmas, along with promises that spring would come early that year, and I could get out and ride it. Well, that hadn't happened yet. I was hoping that by the time we were back home from Auntie Kathy's that the snow'd be gone. It was the end of April, but our lawn was still solid white and the street in front of our house was really icy. Worse than that, it was cold. Way too cold to be out riding a new mountain bike. The vandals had slashed both of the thick-treaded tires, taken off the seat and somehow bent the frame.

That's what stupid Mark reminds me of in this place when he cuts the rusty padlock off the latch and kicks open the door instead've just turning the knob and walking in. He wrecks things for the sake of wrecking things. And for the sake of impressing Nikki, of course. Boys will hold their breath until they turn purple to get Nik's attention.

I wait outside for a bit on that sloping veranda, breathing in the salt air, letting them go on ahead. Our cousin Derek is with us, my Auntie Cindy's son, my age but obnoxious. When we first moved here with Mom, we stayed with them for a bit, then we moved in with Grammie. I like Grammie's house way more than Derek's. Auntie Cindy's nice to me, but I think she can be kind of mean to Mom. They're sisters.

"You comin', Charly Pederson? Or are you chicken?" Derek calls out to me from inside the dark hall.

"I'm not chicken, I'm just looking around out here. Is that *okay* with you?"

At the far end of the veranda, two chains, different lengths, hang and swing in the wind. Out here, on the island, lots of old houses have porch swings, and I wonder if one used to hang from those chains. Back in Alberta, my best friend Allie had a swing, but it was mounted on a metal frame and sat in their backyard. We had some good laughs on that swing.

A railing runs most of the way around that veranda.

It stops dead where it's broken away, maybe from the weather and time, or maybe by other vandals like Mark. How could you know? I always want to know stuff like that. What things used to be like and how they got to be the way they are now. Mom says I'd like studying history, but when they show us those videos about Louis Riel and Cape Breton coal mining in Social Studies, I know she's wrong.

I step into the dark hall and stand there just inside the door, letting my eyes get used to the gloom. I hear Nikki's voice first.

"I don't like this place, Mark. And anyway, the bell's going to go soon. We should be getting back."

"Naw. We've got lots of time. What're you afraid of? I'm right here."

Then it's Derek's turn. "Oh, brother. Knock it off, will you? That's just gross."

I know what is going on, and I'm glad I'm still safe in the hallway. For a moment, I actually catch myself feeling sorry for Derek, having to watch them kiss. Getting used to the dark, I can see a dusty staircase to my right, its banister clogged with cobwebs. I wonder if Nikki saw these when she came in? I don't mind spiders, but they freak her out. Bad. Heading down the hall and following the sound of their voices, I find them in the kitchen.

"Hey, chicken. You made it in."

"Shut up, Derek."

"Dark in here." This is Mark's brilliant observation. He thinks that because he's in Grade Eleven, he automatically knows everything. Nikki's boyfriend

4

swaggers over to one of the kitchen windows and gives the yellowed, brittle shade a hard tug. It rolls up with a snap! and a burst of dust. Now we can better see what the place looks like. It's like lots of kitchens I've seen in prairie museums on summer vacations—only less lived-in. But that's more the smell than the look. The air's stale, kind of like the air in our garden shed back home when it got really hot out.

There's a counter, pretty low, and a deep sink with a few black spots where the enamel was chipped away. There's a fridge, a broom and dustpan in the corner, a square wooden table and four chairs. Everything has a layer of dust on it, and Derek is busy writing his name and drawing silly faces on every surface with his finger.

Mark lets out a low whistle. "Check this." He points near the black and silver wood-burning stove with his free hand, the one not clutching Nikki's waist. "The rocking chair's right there—just like they say."

"Who says?" Nikki asks, looking around the room as if expecting something to leap out at her from the shadows.

"Everybody round here. That's who. You haven't heard the story of the O'Leary house?" Mark talks about it like it's world famous. Grammie told me the story, but Stupid's already launching into it, so I'll have to hear it again. Good story—when Grammie told it.

"You like ghost stories?" she asked me, handing me a steaming mug of tea, sweet with sugar. We were at Grammie's kitchen table the Monday after we'd moved in there, and I'd just got back from school. It'd been a better

5

day than I'd been having so far. Maybe Mom was right. Maybe things would get easier after I'd settled in a bit. Grammie had a deck of cards lying on the plastic tablecloth between us. She was going to teach me to play Queens.

"Sure. There are ghosts around here?" She'd got me curious.

"Are there ghosts?" Grammie sat down across from me. "Charly girl, you can't imagine! There're stories up and down this Island about ghosts and goblins and about things folks just can't explain." She leaned toward me. "Strange things. Spooky things."

"I don't care so much about ghosts from other places, but what about from right here? In your town? You got ghosts right here?"

"Well, yes. Of course, there're ghosts from around here. I used to know one of them." She sipped her tea, watching me over the rim of her mug.

"What?"

"Mmm-hmm. I used to be friends with a current ghost when she wasn't yet a ghost—before she died, that is."

"No way."

"Oh, yes way."

"How'd she die then?"

"Murdered. Thrown down a well. I sure did miss her after it happened." With that, Grammie gave a long sigh and started to deal. "Okay, dear, we each get eight cards. Your sister joining us, or is she going to stay up in her room?"

"Grammie!"

"What? What's the problem?"

"You can't just tell me that you were friends with a ghost and then play cards! You're making it up anyway. You're just teasing."

"No. I'm certainly not." But I could tell she was trying not to smile. Grammie's nice, but she thinks she's funny. She stopped dealing. Three cards lay in front of me face down. "Want to hear the whole story? It takes awhile, and I can't tell it and play cards at the same time. I take both my cards and my storytelling too seriously to play and talk. So which will it be?"

Two

Mark saunters up to the rocking chair, gives it a big tug backward then lets it rock violently back and forth.

"Mark. Don't," Nikki scolds.

"Why not? What's the matter with you?" He sets his foot on the curved wood where the legs end, and the chair stops rocking. "That better, princess?"

"Hey, look!" With a long creak, Derek lifts the heavy lid of the woodbox tucked in by the stove. "There's still wood in here!" He reaches in and pulls out a dry log, bits of ancient bark falling onto the worn linoleum.

"Give me that, four eyes." Mark grabs the log from my cousin and throws it against the wall beside the door leading in from that dark hall. It leaves a fresh gash in the old flooring where it lands.

"You're such a jerk, Mark! Can't we just look around without you wrecking everything?" Nikki stands with her hands on her hips, glaring at the tall, skinny guy she'd hooked up with the first week we'd got to PEI. I figure he won't last long. Good thing, too.

I lean in the next archway, the one that joins the kitchen with the back sitting room. "It's true, Mark." He looks at me levelly. "You're acting like a jerk." I turn away from him and walk into what Grammie would call the parlour. Nikki follows, and all of a sudden, it feels kinda like girls against boys.

On their way out of the kitchen, one of them, probably Mark, slams the woodbox lid shut. I jump, and most likely so does Nikki, but neither of us says anything. We just pretend we don't notice.

"How come the furniture's all covered up?" my sister asks anyone who wants to answer, reaching out to lift a corner of one sheet. She peeks beneath it. "Wow. This is really nice."

"Take the stupid sheet off already." With a mighty sweep of his arm, Mark has the sheet lying in a heap on the floor. Now we can see the old-fashioned sofa. It's red, and its fabric feels like velvet under my fingers.

This room is as dusty as the kitchen. We can't see as well, because the thick curtains over all the windows are drawn, but we can see clouds of dust rising from the sheets that Mark is pulling off the stuff in the sitting room. Pretty soon, all the furniture is bare, and a heap of white sheets lies in the middle of the room on the large braided rug.

"Come and check this out." Mark yanks the cover off an old pump organ.

Nikki runs her hand with its pink-painted nails over the smooth wood finish. She always talked about taking music lessons and started piano lessons one time, but quit. "I wish we had this at home."

"We've got that piano in the basement. You could ask my mom and maybe use it," Derek offers. Even he's trying to impress Nik. I want to gag. Or maybe he's just trying to be nice. It's hard to tell with him. Anyway, Nikki ignores his suggestion.

Then without warning, and for no reason at all, Mark, who's been wandering around the room touching everything, strides up and viciously kicks the old organ, leaving a deep scar with his hiking boot. It groans under his abuse.

"What did you do that for, you jerk!" Nikki yells at him.

Mark just laughs. "It's old stuff, princess. It don't belong to nobody. Lighten up." Then, as if to make his point understood, he kicks the organ again. With that, Nikki turns and walks out, back into the kitchen.

Mark follows her. "Hey! Don't be like that! What's the big deal, anyway? Nobody cares."

Derek and I can hear them arguing in the kitchen, but we tune them out. I walk over to one of the tall windows and pull aside the heavy curtain, its fabric a darker red than the material on the sofa. The window pane is really dusty, but beyond it, the bright sun reflects off the water of Northumberland Strait. Behind me, I hear my cousin approach, footsteps falling softly on the wood floor.

"See, Derek? The house looks out over the strait. Nice view, eh?"

"What's that?" My cousin answers me from where he stands way across the room, still examining the damage Mark has done to the elegant old instrument. In his hand he holds a sheaf of sheet music, which he seems to be trying to decipher. A chill runs up my spine. I'm sure I heard him walking up behind me.

"Uh…I said that you should come look out this window. It's a nice view of the strait." I swallow hard then ask, "Derek? How long you been standing there?"

"I dunno. About as long as you've been over there, I guess. Hey. That is a great view. Bet you can see the ghost ship good from here. And look. That's the well they talk about. Grammie mention that to you? She likes the story. Says she knew that woman before she died."

"Yeah. She told me. Doesn't make this place seem any less spooky," I confide to him. The moment the words are out, I regret them.

He turns on me. "I knew it! You *are* a chicken! I bet you didn't even want to come in here!"

"It's not that I'm chicken, Derek. It's an old house. That makes it creepy, that's all."

I try to reason with him, but he's already making chicken noises, his hands tucked up under his armpits and flapping his elbows. "Bock…b…b…bock!"

"You're an idiot."

"Bock! Bock! Bock!"

"Whatever."

Finally, Derek gets bored and stops making his chicken sounds. I let the curtains fall closed again, and he grabs a handful of the heavy material, bunches it up and lays it on the wide sill. This makes a little space in between the curtain for the light to get in. Nikki and Mark are quiet in the kitchen. Apparently, they've made up. I walk away and sit down on the sofa.

Derek comes and sits down beside me. Apparently, he wants to make up, too.

"Comfy," I say.

"Yup. Sure is," Derek agrees.

I sit in the middle of the couch, Derek to my right. I'm about to get up and take a closer look at some of the neat stuff that fills the room when I feel someone else sit down to my left. I even hear the couch springs sigh under someone's weight, feel the cushions sink.

"Derek? Did you feel that?"

"Feel what?"

"It felt like someone just sat down beside me."

"*I'm* sitting beside you," he says impatiently. I think I'm scaring him, and it would be funny if I wasn't so scared myself.

"No. Right here." Cautiously, I point to my left.

He leans forward and peers around me. "I don't see anything."

"Neither do I. That's not what I said." Why am I whispering? Whatever the reason, my cousin has started to, as well.

"Char." I look at his face blanching white. "Look at the cushion."

There beside me is a noticeable indent. It *looks* like someone is sitting there, their weight pushing in the seat of the sofa. We both shoot up with something like an electric jolt, Derek nearly tripping over the oval coffee table, and me nearly tripping over Derek as we scramble to get away from that sofa.

We bolt through the archway into the kitchen, past Nikki and Mark, leaning there together by the low counter. Derek's in the lead, and I am close on his heels.

"What happened? Where're you two going?" Nikki calls after us. It's as if running is contagious, because they both dash out after us. I don't remember touching the stairs off the veranda. I think I leap straight down all four, meeting Derek at the bottom, where we place our hands on our knees and gasp for breath.

"You guys see something?" Mark pries. At least he closed the door when he left the house. Probably doesn't want to get into trouble. Or maybe he's afraid that whatever Derek and I are running from will come running through that open door and snatch him right off the lawn. I caught my breath first, and so I answer.

"Not exactly."

"What do you mean, 'not exactly'? Either you did or you didn't. Which one is it?"

"I guess by your definition, we didn't see anything, okay, Mark? Happy?" My heart's finally slowing down.

"That's what I thought." He sounds unimpressed. "Come on, Nik. Bell's gonna go soon." Nikki and her boyfriend walk on ahead of us. We all walk quickly, worried that the afternoon bell will ring before we make it back to the schoolyard.

"That was kinda freaky, wasn't it?" Derek ventures.

"Yeah, it was. Are you sure about the sofa? I mean, it was pretty dark. Was the sofa seat really pushed in, like someone was sitting there?"

Then, clear as anything, we hear a baby cry. Not a soft sound, but something more like wailing. Derek and I freeze in our tracks, both of us looking over our shoulders at the window above the veranda—the open one.

13

Three

The sun hasn't quite risen yet when I wake up feeling guilty about going into that old house. I dreamed that the owner was there watching us, tied up in a chair and gagged while we broke in. Well, *I* didn't break in. Mark did that, but I went along with it. Mom would say that's just as bad. That's why I didn't tell her.

In my little bedroom upstairs in Grammie's house, I pull on my jeans and a sweater. It feels cold this morning, but outside my window, beyond that maple tree, the sky is blue, even without the sun, which means the day will feel like summer by the afternoon. Only the morning gives away fall's secret. That third step creaks when my foot hits it, and I pause for a second, listening for Mom or Grammie. I don't hear anything, no rustle of sheets or sleepy sighs, so I move to the fourth step, and I'm on my way. Grammie's house is huge, especially compared to where we lived back in Alberta. I shared a room with Nikki there, even though we had three bedrooms. The last one was kept empty and dustless in case company ever came.

Here there are four bedrooms upstairs, one for each

of us. My room is small, with lots of Grammie's stuff still in it, but it's my own space. This house is where Mom grew up with my Aunt Cindy and their two brothers. One brother, my Uncle Bruce, lives down in the States. Boston, I think. I met him once a long time ago, but I don't really remember him. He never got married and doesn't have any kids. Uncle Gary, Mom's youngest brother, died, but nobody talks about it, so I don't know how or even when. It must've been a long time ago, because I don't remember it, and I'm thirteen.

Downstairs, I click on the light above the stove and pick up the pad of coloured paper that Grammie keeps by the phone. I don't want everyone to wake up and worry, so I leave a note:

Dear Mom and Grammie, I'm not in bed because I'm outside trying to find some bugs for science class. I'll probably be back for breakfast.
  Love,
  Charly

From down in the cupboard by the toaster, I bring out an empty peanut butter jar (Grammie saves everything! It drives Mom crazy), punch some holes in the red plastic lid with a knife and head out.

Before I'm halfway across Grammie's yard, the tips of my running shoes are soaked right through to my socks, and I feel wet on my toes. I like the smell of the dew-drenched grass and the way the morning feels on my skin, chilly but soft. The birds are just starting to wake up as I walk, and they twitter at me from high in the trees. A nice sound, not like the blue jay screeching at me, making me jump. I look up when she flies out from behind her shield of red, yellow and orange leaves, and see that her feathers are a bluer blue than the sky.

I move off the road and into the ditch, where I pick a bunch of grass to stuff inside my peanut butter jar, thereby creating a bug habitat. On a sapling on the other side of the ditch, I find a couple of ladybugs. I guide them onto my index finger and into my jar. I stay in the deep ditch, the bottoms of my jeans dark with dew, and walk along, scanning the plants there for something other than ladybugs. Mr. Neillson had said that we were to find a variety if we could. Doesn't seem possible, not at that hour, anyway, and not where I'm looking. So I keep on walking, the birds keep on singing, and pretty soon, the sun peeks over the horizon, changing the sky from bluey-grey to pink.

I reach that tiny knoll on the outside of town, and the O'Leary house on Northumberland Strait suddenly looms before me. Later, after everything has happened and I'm home safe, I'll think that maybe I'd been planning to go back to the house all along. But now, when it seems to pop up there, I feel surprised. I've walked a long way and haven't found any more bugs. There isn't a rush. They aren't due until Monday, and the day I've ended up at the house on purpose accidentally is Friday. I have the whole weekend.

The strait stretches out behind that big old mansion, empty and still, and I keep walking through the knee-high grass until I'm at the gate. It hangs there by one good hinge, the other looking like it had rusted right through a long time ago. It isn't latched. It wasn't when we were here yesterday, and we never latched it as we left, so now it sits crooked and wide open. It's funny to see that gate, because there's barely any fence left standing, its thick posts rotted and fallen, the wire mesh buried in years of tangled grass. The gate itself is attached to metal poles, and I guess that's why it still stands straighter than the fence. I stand here for a minute or two, one hand on the lopsided gate, browned by time, while my other hand grips the peanut butter jar. I set my home for wayward ladybugs in the tall grass outside the fence and step through the gate.

Strange. I blink once, then a second time. On this side of the dilapidated gate, the sky seems brighter, the house whiter and the strait wider. I smile, remembering how my Grade Six class last year back home roared with laughter at the story I wrote to read to the class. I was so nervous! But once I was up at the front of the room, reading as best I could, and heard the first snicker, not *at* me, but *because* of me, it was easy! It was even *fun!* I always had friends, people to hang out with, but I was never really popular or unpopular. Just there. Not a class clown, that's for sure. The story was about a heart transplant on a chicken—only the heart had belonged to a beaver, so now the chicken acted like a beaver. Miss Sunders gave me an A+, but what I liked better was that she laughed, too, loud enough for everyone in the class to hear. That was the best day.

Now the sky brightens, along with the old house's paint job, and I'm impressed again by my imagination. Really impressed. Maybe this will make a good story someday. "Old House Turns Brand New Before Imaginative Kid's Eyes".

I feel stone under my runners, flat and solid, not all crumbly and crunchy like it was yesterday. The grass seems shorter now, and I can see boxes of red flowers on the steps, flowers I never noticed when I was standing outside the fence. They're pretty and full, like flowers are in the fall, and hard to miss.

I've never been very brave. I don't like breaking into old buildings or egging passing cars at Halloween or lipping off the kids in Grade Nine. But I'm not scared when I step up onto the white porch, straight and unsagging, and reach out for the doorknob. There's no latch, no padlock, and the knob glints in the sun, dent and rust free. I turn it, and it doesn't screech. Instead, the door swings open smoothly without creaking. Weird. My imagination's obviously improving with age and experience.

"Hello?" No answer. I step over the threshold and notice right away that the dust and cobwebs are gone from the wooden banister. Each stair looks polished, and the spacious entry smells like lemons. There's a narrow table with spindly legs on the right hand side of the entry, sitting tight up against the wall made by the staircase after it turns and begins its steady ascent. An unlit lamp sits on top, the stained glass shade reflecting the light coming in through the open door. "Hello?" I say it again and listen hard, but I don't move from where I stand just inside the door. When I hear a voice echoing mine, I jump.

"Hello?" The word sounds crackly and dry, like fall leaves lying deep along the curbs during those first days back to school. I stop dead, can't move. It feels like I've stepped into wet cement that's hardening fast. That's how she finds me, wide-eyed and with my tongue stuck firmly to the roof of my mouth. She moves from the kitchen and stands beneath the archway leading into the hallway, a thick book clutched in one hand. The woman wears a blue skirt that ends right about her knees, and a cream-coloured blouse made of shiny material. Around her neck and lying against her collarbone is a string of pearls. I'm frozen, too scared at being caught in the house even to shake, and I forget to breathe until I feel my lungs tighten and beg for air. Then I gulp.

Her free hand moves up to her hip and rests there on her narrow black belt. "So. You've come back to see me, have you?"

I swallow hard.

"Yeah. I…guess." What does she mean, "back"? Had she seen us yesterday? Was she actually inside the house watching, or had she been outside as we broke in or as we made our hasty retreat? Either way, she's smiling, and that's a good sign. Surprise.

"Well, why don't you come in, since you're already here." The woman, reminding me a bit of my own mom (except much taller), indicates the book she holds in her left hand. I see that her index finger marks her place. "I was just doing some reading." She laughs lightly, adding, "Seems I do a lot of that lately. Glad to have company. It's been awhile." She points her chin in the direction of the kitchen behind her, beckoning me to follow, and turns neatly on the highish heel of her black shoe. I follow on legs that have become unstuck but are as wobbly as a baby giraffe's.

"Would you like tea?" she asks, setting the hefty book down on the counter. Her auburn hair is brushed out to her shoulders. It picks up the light that streams brightly through the kitchen window.

"Sure—please."

"Go ahead. Sit down." She points one of her slender hands at the wooden table, painted white, with four chairs around it, all pushed in tidily. A bit reluctantly, I pull one out and sit down, my eyes focussing for a second on the fat red and blue diamonds on the tablecloth. No dust. No shadows. The elegant lady looks over her shoulder, and when she smiles at me, those little lines around her eyes remind me of Mom, when she used to be happy. That feels like a long time ago. "What's your name?"

Again I have to swallow before I can talk, prepare my vocal chords to make a sound. Finally, I manage to croak out, "Charly."

"Charly. That's a nice name. Sugar?" Holding a china bowl with a tiny spoon sticking out of it, she looks at me, eyebrows raised above green eyes. I nod. That's the best thing about tea: lots of sugar. It's like this stranger knows me, the way she dumps three spoonfuls into my cup and stirs it round. Mom takes her tea black, but Grammie always has two spoonfuls. She says life is too short not to. Nikki doesn't like tea. She usually wants coffee.

"Do you have a namesake?" I must look kind of blank, because she repeats the same question in a different way. "Are you named after someone?" I was named after someone, but I don't tell a lot of people. I did tell Allie. She threw herself to the carpet and laughed and laughed. At first, I laughed too. But she guffawed too long, and I started to feel angry. "Shut up!" She thought I was kidding and kept on clutching her stomach and kicking her feet. "I said shut up!" I nudged her hard in the ribs with my foot and went home, leaving her there in her basement lying in front of the TV. She called later that night and said that I should be proud of my name, because I'd been named after a hero. That was a good thing, no matter what the name. It was the only fight we'd ever had.

I was sketchy on the details regarding the heroic act itself. There'd been a strike at a coal mine in Saskatchewan. The workers had been living in these shacks, lining the walls with newspaper in winter to keep the wind and snow out. The houses had stoves made out of barrels, but most times, the miners didn't have enough wood or coal to keep warm. The workers paid high rent on these shacks and bought groceries from the mining company's store on credit—using up their paycheques before they even got paid! Everything they needed was sold in that store, and it was all really expensive. The mining company controlled everyone, and as my mom told me, kept them poor.

"My Grandpa Nordestrom. I was named after my grandpa." I hear the hesitation in my answer, yet I tell the lady the truth. I don't have to. Could've lied. She would've never known.

She doesn't bat an eye, just says, "That's unusual. Let's go into the parlour, where it's comfortable." With both hands, she carries a silver tray with our cups on it and a plate of cookies. Fancy. "Putting on the dog" is what Grammie would say. I get up and follow her, remembering to push my chair back in. I sit down on that brocade couch in the very same spot I'd sat with Derek the day before, less than twenty-four hours ago. There are tall tables with round, polished tops on either end of the chesterfield that I could swear weren't there last time I sat down. There's also a rug upon which all this furniture sits, the two chairs included. I spot a big gap on the tightly packed bookshelves between the tall windows and wonder if the book lying there in the kitchen accounts for the empty space.

My host hands me my cup, steam rising, and sets the tray on the oval table in the centre of the burgundy and black area rug, the kind Dad wouldn't let us walk on if it were in our house back home. In fact, he probably wouldn't want kids in this room at all. Way too nice in here. She sits down across from me in the chair closest to the windows and bookshelves, crossing her legs. She sure looks dressed up.

"Your grandpa's name wasn't Charly." It sounds like she's been thinking about my name, how a man couldn't be a Charly.

At first, I was scared snotless by this lady, because I

didn't expect her to be here. The house seemed deserted and rundown the day before, but already she seems not a bit scary. Just like a normal woman. I tell her, "My grandpa's name was Charlie, so my parents softened the 'ch' to say 'shh' and made a name for me." I think I sound proud of it. I suppose I am.

She nods and smiles, her eyes going crinkly again. "How interesting!" I can tell she means it, so I tell her the other story that goes with my name.

"My sister Nikki is named after my Grandpa McNickle. His name was Nicholas. On her birth certificate, it actually *says* Nicholas. Maybe Mom and Dad wanted boys to give these names to, but they got us. Two girls."

"Looking at you, I bet they're so happy to have daughters." She passes me the plate of cookies. "Want one?"

"Sure." It's kind of weird to be eating cookies for breakfast, but hey, it would be impolite to refuse. I dunk the ladyfinger in my tea and transfer it quickly to my mouth, not letting one drop land on my clothes or on the couch. When she does the same, I grin. "I like the way you eat cookies. Like a kid."

"Oh, I don't eat kids." Her smile's gone, and she studies my face.

I gotta admit, for a minute I think she's serious, then her face breaks into brightness again. I laugh.

"Sure you don't. Not for breakfast, anyway." She laughs, too, and takes another cookie after offering me a second. As I munch on the cookie, I let my eyes roam around, over the lamps, doilies, paintings and through the archway that separates the dining room from the parlour the way a similar, narrower archway divides the kitchen from this sitting room. When the tall grandfather clock on the far side of the dining room strikes its commanding tone, a jolt shoots through me.

The lady with the pearls and the cookies notices this. "You don't have a clock at home?"

"Not like that one! That thing could wake the dead!" That's what Grammie says when we've got our stereos or the TV up too loud: "You girls are going to wake the dead!"

She just smiles. "I wish that were true." Then she glances over her shoulder and out one of the tall windows overlooking the strait before turning quickly back to me. "More tea?"

"Naw. Too much makes me hyper."

"You're a little on the high-strung side as it is, aren't you?" I can tell she's not trying to be mean. It's something she's noticed about me, and it happens to be true.

"Yup. I am." I shrug. "You sure got a nice house. How long've you lived here?"

"I'm not sure now. But before, when I shared the house with Robert, my husband, we were here almost six years. Those were long, long years—" She looks at me suddenly then, like adults do when they've said something they shouldn't maybe have said in front of kids. But I'm not a kid any more. I'm a teenager, a teenager who's heard and watched my parents bicker and fight for over half my life. I want to tell her, want to say that I know about marriages. Lots of times when Mom was angry, she'd talk to me about Dad, warn me about getting married. And sometimes Dad talked to me, told me not to turn out like my Mom, to do something with my life so I wouldn't blame everyone else for how everything turned out for me. But I don't tell her I feel mostly grown-up or that I understand imperfect marriages. Instead, I blurt, "My parents hate each other."

Her green eyes widen, and her lips part. Her teacup stops on its way to her mouth. "Oh? Why do you say that?"

"They told me they do. That's why I say it." I set my flowered cup on the oval table and stretch my arms over my head. "Well, I oughta get going. Mom's gonna wonder where I am."

She sets her cup down too, but on the silver tray, the porcelain making a little clank against the metal. I like that sound. It reminds me of eating out and of Christmas Eve communion, where they pass around those stacked trays full of holes, each holding a tiny glass three-quarters full of grape juice. Last Christmas, our last one as a family, Nikki called it doing shooters for the Lord. Mom laughed, and Dad got mad. He said it was sacrilegious—whatever that means. I didn't even know what a shooter was.

We stand up at the same time, and she says, "Well, thanks for dropping in this evening. It was a nice visit."

"Yeah, it was."

I walk behind her as she leads the way through the kitchen area and back down the hall, leaving the tray on the coffee table. Then I think about what she said, so I ask, "Evening?"

She hesitates and glances back at me, the click of her

heels stopping. "It's eight thirty. Later, even." She looks confused, and I guess to her, I probably look the same. I stare for a moment, catch myself and blink. I put my hand out, grasping the doorknob. Yesterday, it felt loose. Today, it's secure.

"Well, thanks for the tea."

"Will you come back some time? For another visit?" The woman inclines her head toward me, as if she's listening intently for my answer, like something depends on that answer.

"Sure. I guess." I turn the knob and open the door. "See ya!" I call this over my shoulder, my runners already on the long, white boards of the wide veranda. Then I think to ask, "What's your name?"

"Katherine. Katherine O'Leary."

Katherine's nice, and I liked talking to her, felt comfortable with her. Still, it feels good to get out of that house, to hear the door finally close behind me. I walk out across the lawn and onto the road leading back home. My shoes, that had mostly dried during my time at the O'Leary house, become soaked again almost as soon as they touch the grass outside her yard. Yet the grass seemed dry within that tumbled-down fence. Weird. I turn around, walking backwards for a bit down that paved road, and pause when my eyes focus back in on the O'Leary place. I shade my eyes with my left hand and blink hard twice.

Suddenly, the house looks grey and weathered against the bright, morning sky above Northumberland Strait. A gull swoops down low over its slightly bowed roofline, and chains dangle where moments ago there had hung a wooden swing built for two.

Another surprise greets me when I get in the door at home. According to the clock on the stove, I've been gone for just over half an hour. Everyone is still sound asleep.

Four

When I wake up on Saturday morning, I smell bacon frying and hear Grammie filling the kettle at the kitchen sink. Stretching, I note that the sky beneath the partially-raised bedroom shade is leaden grey. A winter sky. Already. Half-asleep, I remember my dream, the one I'd just had. My dad was here at Grammie's, and I'd run in the front door after my visit with Katherine. I couldn't help myself. I told him all about her, how I didn't know if she was real or a ghost. He stood there, staring as the story fell in pieces out of me, broken, disjointed syllables. When I faltered he broke in, telling me: *Charly, you can't spend your life daydreaming. You'll never get anywhere. Why don't you join some sports team or something? Get outside, get some fresh air. Sitting around in that room of yours reading and drawing. Where's that gonna get you? You'll end up crazy like your grandmother.*

That's when I woke up, smelled breakfast cooking, heard the tap running, the pipes creaking and sighing. Dad's image, tall and frowning, faded. In real life, he'd never told me to stop daydreaming, but I kinda felt like he'd wanted me to. I don't know. You can't know what people are thinking. But he did say more than once, right in front of Nik and me, that Grammie was crazy. Mom would be telling us a story about Grammie, something from when Mom was still a kid living on the Island, and Dad would say, "Oh, c'mon, Sylvia. You know your mother's crazy." Mom wouldn't answer him, but her face would go stony, and she wouldn't smile again for the rest of the day.

Soon as I reach the bottom of the staircase, Grammie greets me from the stove. "Mornin', missy." Her back's to me, her apron cinched up so tight she looks like the pictures in my science text of cells dividing, pinching themselves into two halves, finally forming two new individuals. "Long sleep. Rest well?"

"Yes. Thanks. How 'bout you?" I sit down in the chair closest to the stairs.

"Not as long as you, but I'd bet deeper."

"Morning, Nik." My sister is circling around the big table like a pouting bird, setting four places with plates and cutlery. She passes close by the back of my chair and with a lot of effort replies, "Morning."

Grammie turns from the stove, moves to the kitchen sink, rinses her hands and wipes them briskly on her apron. She opens the fridge and brings out a glass pitcher half-full of orange juice. "Okay, girls. It's ready. Charly, would you call your mom? This morning she claimed this kitchen isn't big enough for the two of us, so she went outside to rake leaves."

Nikki flops down. I stand up and walk through the

living room to the front door. Only the storm door's closed, its glass pane foggy from the heat of Grammie's cooking meeting the cool morning air. I open it, and Mom turns at the creak its hinges make, the sun shining off her hair, hair the same golden colour as Nikki's.

"Breakfast's ready!" I call across the lawn to where she's raking leaves, yellow, orange and red, into a huge heap beneath the maple tree. Mom leans the rake up against the tree, pulls off her gardening gloves, and gripping them in her hand, walks toward the house.

I hold the storm door open for her, and she touches my shoulder for a second as she brushes by. "Thanks, hon." She doesn't look at me. Sometimes, nowadays, she makes me feel invisible. Most of the time.

After breakfast, Mom goes back outside and, because Nik helped make breakfast, I help Grammie with the dishes while my sister reads her fashion magazines in Grammie's back porch, the sun porch. There isn't much to do, really. I just have to rinse off the plates and put them in the dishwasher as Grammie clears everything off the table. Then she washes the frying pans, pot and spatula, and I dry them. By now, I've learned where everything fits into her crammed cupboards. Everything, pots, pans, plates, jugs and jars, set together as deliberately as jigsaw puzzle pieces.

Grammie tugs the plug, and I watch her swish the bit of soapy water around to clear out the grease and bits of egg from the sink. Her steely grey hair is a fuzzy mass about four centimetres tall that remains motionless while she works. I imagine that a good, stiff shore wind could flatten it against her head, but nothing else.

"Grammie, I was wondering..." I'm not sure how to ask this, since I told her before that I didn't want to hear *all* the stories she had to tell.

My grandmother's hand stops moving in the sink. "What? You ready to hear some stories?" she guesses and looks at me closely, as if she's trying to gauge how interested I really am.

I shrug and tilt the dish rack, watching rivulets of clear water move down its deep ridges to splash down into the bottom of the sink. "Yeah. I guess. Maybe." She waits until I glance up from my chore and our eyes meet before she answers my question. She looks grave, as if I'd just asked her if she ever killed a man with her bare hands.

"Well, I suppose we could do 'the tour.'" Grammie hangs the towel over the stove door handle. She unties her apron as she sticks her head around the corner into the sun porch. "Nikki, your sister and I are going for a drive. You want to come along?"

I hear her reply, "No. Thanks, though." Nikki is never as polite with Mom or me as she is with Grammie.

"All right then. See you later. We won't be long."

"Where're we going?" I speak to her back as she strides to the wide front closet with its double doors. When we first arrived here in August, I remember being so impressed by the front entry. Wood panelling on the bottom half, yellow and pink flowery wallpaper on the top. That day, when she'd noticed me admiring the little glass chandelier and the hexagonal glass window above the door, Grammie told me, "Twelve-foot ceiling in here. The rest of the downstairs rooms all have ten-foot. Upstairs, eight."

I recall thinking, "This lady doesn't know how to talk to kids." Since then, I've changed my mind. Maybe she's learned how to talk, or maybe I've learned how to listen. Who knows? Whatever it is, though, we've got lots to say to each other. Some days, if it wasn't for Grammie, I wouldn't be talking to anyone in this house.

Grammie rests her right hand casually on the steering wheel, the driver's side window wide open. On the way out of the house, following the sidewalk to the long, unpaved driveway that runs alongside the house, she called out to Mom, "Sylvia! Charly's asked about ghosts. I'm going to take her on the grand tour. Shouldn't be longer than an hour."

"Okay!" Mom lifted a gardening glove clad hand then stopped mid-wave, adding, "Charly, don't believe a word she tells you."

We drive slowly in Grammie's big old car, the sun reflecting off the polished dash and me sinking into the velour seat, a split armrest separating driver and passenger. I push down on one of the chrome buttons on the door, and all four doors lock simultaneously with a clean click. "It's the other one," Grammie informs me, and as I depress the second button, my window slides down. I stick my arm out and feel the wind wrap it up cool. Grammie doesn't tell me to bring it back inside. Instead, she sticks hers out straight, as far as it will go. Even when a potato truck rumbles by, she keeps her arm defiantly outstretched, just daring fate and the heavy vehicle to lop off her limb. The old man behind the wheel smiles and waves, the green cap he wears pulled down so far, I wonder how he can see the road. When she finally brings her arm in, it's so she can turn the radio on. I hate Grammie's country music but know better than to whine about it. Nikki dared once, and Grammie just turned it up. Now it's playing softly, and we can chat over it, no problem.

"You see that grove of trees up there on the left?" We're out of town, the fields spreading out around us in all directions, always ending at the Atlantic Ocean. There's nothing else they can do. Everything stops for the water. Until the bridge was built, that is. Now cars and people disregard the cold, grey water. Can't even see it from the bridge. Grammie is showing me a forest. Well, not like an Alberta forest, but a pretty big bunch of trees. Big enough that I can't see for sure where it ends or quite how far back from the road and away from the shore it extends. "One winter, seven folks went into that grove."

When she pauses, I ask, "So?" It's exactly what she wants. Dad always said she was melodramatic. Maybe because she sometimes sets me up like this.

"None came out."

"They all went in together? In a group?"

Grammie glances over at me, her lips pressed into a straight, tight line, and nods slowly.

"As if!"

She doesn't reply to my scoffing, only shrugs and reaches for the volume knob.

"Wait," I break in before she turns that awful music up. "Why didn't anybody come out?"

Satisfied that I'm paying attention, Grammie's arm returns to the safety armrest—my safety, that is. She slows the car and pulls onto the narrow shoulder. "See in there? A little past that gate?"

"What gate?" I lean forward and try to see past her out the driver's side window. Again she points.

"See those two posts? Bigger than the others? There's a gate right in through there."

"Kind of behind that branch? I see it now. What were they doing anyway?"

"Folks say they were hunting rabbits. Headed out as the sun was just starting to go down. No one ever heard a shot fired—but they found their rifles, their lanterns and half a flask of whiskey the next day, all hanging suspended by binder twine from the branches of a big old maple tree." Grammie clucks her tongue behind her teeth like she does when she thinks something's senseless. "No one goes in those woods any more. I imagine the rabbits are happy." She eases her big car into gear, and we roll back onto the deserted road.

I recognize most of the winding roads we drive down but not any of the stories she tells. All of them are news to me. Lots about curses, unexplained disappearances, people turning into trees and rocks. Most of them are pretty unconvincing, and sound a lot like the type of stories people from small places make up for entertainment. I don't think I believe, but I don't think anyone could ever get me to venture through that gate and into those dark woods, either. I don't want to be part of the next generation's folklore: the Alberta girl who disappeared into the woods, her glasses found hanging from a birch tree.

After we pass two cemeteries and the last place the ghost train had been spotted, the tangle of twisted roads leads again to the outskirts of town, though this time to the edge of town closest to the strait and to Miss Katherine's house. Grammie slows the car as we get closer to the house then pulls off to the side of the road. As she puts the car in park and turns off the ignition, she explains, "When I was about nine or ten, a little younger than you, I used to visit the woman who lived here."

The engine tick-ticks in the silence. Grammie takes a deep breath and settles back into her seat. "She came here in May of 1952 to set up house with the man she'd just married. He'd lived in that—" Grammie gestures towards the large grey structure "—big old house alone ever since his folks died."

"Where'd she live before coming here? On the Island?"

Grammie shakes her head. "No," she begins slowly, remembering. "I think she came from Halifax. Yes. That's right." She nods, and recollection brightens her eyes. "She talked about going to school in Halifax, about the harbour, about the ships. In some ways, Charly, that city's still a world away from here. I imagine she missed it, by the way she talked." Grammie sounds more distant when she adds, "I could *feel* the pain in her voice when she told us about it. You know, sometimes it felt as if she wasn't talking to the other girls at all. It was like they just happened to be there, but it was me she wanted to hear her stories, as if it was a history lesson that I specifically needed to know." She gives herself a little shake and comes back to me. "Hmm. Looking back now, she was pretty young then, even though she seemed like such a grown-up to me."

"How old?"

"Twenty-five, probably." Grammie shrugs. "Good age to get married. But I'm not saying it's something you should do, get married that young. Not these days, with other choices." She nudges me without smiling, half-serious. "Well, shall we?" Grammie opens her door and swings a leg out.

"What are you doing?" My voice goes all high and squeaky, and I feel panic settle in my throat.

"I'm gonna go take a look around. We've got plenty of time. You coming?"

I prop open the passenger door and leap out, slamming it heavily. At that, Grammie turns and raises her eyebrows at me, then demonstrates how I should've done it by closing the driver's door firmly but gently. In short strides, she makes her way to the rusty, crooked gate, and I follow behind, feeling my mouth get dry and my limbs go all jelly. At the gate, she bends to pick something up. My bug jar!

"What's this?" Grammie holds the jar up to inspect it more closely. In the light that shines through the glass, I can make out three dead ladybugs lying beneath the wad of browning grass that was green the day I stuffed it in.

"It's mine." I croak out the confession. Man, I need something to drink.

"Yours?" Grammie lowers the jar and looks hard at me, the way I hate. "When were you here?"

Oh, great. Well, here goes…

I tell her about the break-in and about Mark being an idiot. I explain how I wanted to come back, how it felt like someone had been home and watching the whole time we were in the house. The only thing I don't tell her about that day is about the "weight" that sat down between Derek and me on that old sofa. That part of it all seems unbelievable to me. Grammie just listens. She doesn't interrupt or add things in or try to correct me as I talk. In that way, Grammie's a lot different from most adults. When I'm finished and finally empty of words, she nods solemnly and, for some reason, I expect her to head back to the car. Instead, she steps right through the gate. Typical. I'm getting to know her better now.

Five

With Grammie in the lead, we move up those rickety steps and onto the sloping veranda. I glance to my left and notice that the rusty chains that held up the porch swing yesterday are barely moving. Not much wind. When Grammie reaches out and turns it without hesitating, it's clear to me that the doorknob is dented and old. The door opens with a screech, and light floods the entry. It's dusty again, and that abandoned smell is heavy in the air.

"It's been so many years…" Grammie doesn't really say these words so much as she exhales them. "Just look at this place!" She runs her hand over the smooth banister, dust covering it like a wool blanket. Her hand is wrinkled and red and, for just a second, I wonder if my hands will ever look like hers. "It was once so beautiful, Charly. Still is, really. It still feels like a home to me, her home, and it makes me miss her. It's a shame this building's been let go for so long. But easily salvageable if someone ever wanted to do something with it…"

"Shhh—Grammie, listen!" I could swear I just heard a

noise upstairs. Grammie turns to me with alarm mixed with some annoyance, I think, at being told to "shush."

"What? What is it?" She's straining to hear now, too, her head cocked to the right, her hands still and suspended in midair.

"I…I don't know…" I tell her, because I don't, but then the sound comes again, clearer this time, and no mistaking what it is. Crying.

"Someone's here!" With that exclamation, Grammie hollers, "Hello!" and bolts (well, as fast as any grammie can bolt) up the stairs. Now, if I was alone, I'm thinking my reaction may've varied slightly—in that I would've run out the front door and back out that gate without turning around until I was safe in my closet at home. Maybe Grammie *is* a little crazy. Makes you wonder.

So I follow her.

"Grammie!" I whisper at her form ahead of me. "I can't hear it any more."

"Me neither," she assures me without looking over her shoulder. "This ought to be interesting."

What's that supposed to mean?—"interesting"? Scary? Terrifying? Dangerous to a person's health? Just how does my grandmother define "interesting"? Something tells me I'm gonna find out, whether I want to or not.

Suddenly, Grammie stops on the stairs.

"What is it?" The sunlight that had filtered into the entryway and hall hasn't reached around the corner and up these stairs. In the dim light in front of me, it seems that Grammie is looking at something, her head tilted upward. I'm happy enough to stop, wanting to put off meeting up with the crying thing at the top of the stairs. Unless it's Katherine. But if she's here, why hasn't she shown herself yet? Even if she is a ghost, she knows me now. This whole situation just isn't making any sense.

"This painting used to hang above the mantel in the parlour."

Through the gloom, I can just barely make out what Grammie's talking about. Above her, and pretty much where the staircase ends at the second landing, is a huge painting with a gaudy, old-fashioned frame.

"Who are they?"

Grammie reaches up and touches that ugly frame then the picture itself, its dark and uneven surface. Creepy. "His folks. Thomas's. Mr. O'Leary's."

"Katherine's in-laws?"

"Hmm-mm. That's them. Friendly-looking, eh?"

"Not really," I reply, and Grammie laughs. It's still sometimes hard to tell when she's making a joke. Mom calls her sense of humour deadpan. That must mean you can't tell when she's trying to be funny. I don't think it is particularly funny. I don't like those two pairs of hard eyes and two straight mouths that look like they haven't smiled in about a hundred years. Of course, they haven't. Hard to smile when you're dead—unless you're Katherine, that is.

"He was said to be a sea captain, and a prosperous one at that. His wife died years before he did, while Katherine's husband, Thomas, was still a young man and just starting to get into business for himself." Grammie stands there a bit longer, just looking at the picture, finally commenting, "Sure is in good shape. Like new, really." Then she turns and makes her way up the last few stairs. I don't look at that painting as we pass under it, but I shiver. It's like I can feel them watching me. There's a hot patch in the middle of my back, as if their eyes are boring holes into me.

At the top of the stairs, we find ourselves looking down a long dark hall with two tall doors on either side. The first one on our right is wide open. Grammie pops her head in, of course, and exclaims, "Nice bathroom!"

"Nice bathroom?" I can't believe she's excited about a bathroom! We're up here because we heard a weird weeping sound, and now she's enthusiastic about bathroom fixtures. Who cares about plumbing under ordinary circumstances (unless you really need it, like when you're stuck in the car and your parents won't pull over), let alone while we're investigating strange crying.

"Yes. Nice bathroom." She gives me a look that tells me to shut up or get ready for a fight. I know who'll win, so I shut up. "Back in those days, a lot of folks still had outdoor facilities. We did until the sixties. Only the really rich ones got indoor plumbing installed earlier than that. Impressive."

She's serious! To her, this *is* impressive. I can tell by the way she surveys the room from the doorway while I stand watching her. The prospect of snooping through someone's old bathroom isn't even remotely interesting to me, and even though I'm pretty edgy, I'm starting to get a little bored, too. I swear, she touches everything: the tub with feet, the sink on a pedestal, the white wooden chair in the corner beneath the window, even the toilet tank.

Still feeling that burning at my back, I glance over my shoulder and feel all my muscles lurch at the sight of a mouse scuttling away from me down the length of the hall. "You're braver than me, hanging out here," I say.

"What's that?" Grammie has moved the lace curtains aside and is craning her neck first one way then the other, checking out the view of the strait from the "impressive facilities".

"Nothing. Just talking to the inhabitants. Look, shouldn't we be getting back? You told Mom about an hour."

"Yes, yes, I know." Why does she sound like I'm nagging her? Aren't we supposed to be responsible and come home when we say we will? What a double standard. Then she tells me, "We'll get going soon enough. I just want to finish having a quick snoop around—since the door was open and all..." Her voice trails off, and I don't answer. It's clear she intends to look around some more. I give up on the idea of leaving and turn in the bathroom's doorframe to face into the hallway. The light from the open bathroom door makes dusty, pale stabbing motions all around me, thrusting out till it strikes the opposite wall.

Almost right across from where I stand, there's a door, this one closed tight, and further down the passageway, two more doors, one on either side, both closed. Four rooms. I step forward and hit a squeaky part. Is that how it would sound if you stepped on a mouse? Might sound funny, but it would feel gross!—all that skin scooching out and bones breaking, the blood slippery under my shoe.

I take another step, and I'm pretty much halfway to the closed door. We're here now. Might as well have a look. Maybe Katherine'll show up if we stick around. I'll just tell her what Grammie told me: the door was open. And she did tell me to come back any time. So I'm back.

At first, it doesn't feel like the door is going to open. The knob turns all right, with just a bit of a creak, but when I push on it, the door doesn't budge. I press my shoulder up against it and shove with all my weight. The door flies open, and I end up sprawled out on the wood floor on the other side.

"Well, that was graceful. I may be nosey, but at least I'm not uncoordinated." Grammie smiles and holds out her hand. I take it and let her help me up. I can feel my cheeks burning. I can't tell whether I'm feeling mad or embarrassed. Probably both. She must notice, because as I'm brushing the dust from my jeans, she tells me, "I'm teasing you, Charly."

"I know." But her words don't sound like an apology. Instead, it sounds like she's correcting me. I'm starting to see where Mom gets it from.

Grammie gasps, and I look up quickly, thinking maybe she's seen Katherine. "So this is it. This is the room. Oh, it's so sad. You can *feel* it, can't you?"

I can. The whole room feels heavy or depressed or something. Being in here makes me feel dark on the inside.

"Look at the crib and the rocker! That teddy bear

and the fire engine! Everything's been left just as if…"

"As if what?" I stare at Grammie, waiting for an explanation. For a moment there, I don't think she's going to let me in on it. She looks at me then, and I wish she'd tell me what's going on.

Grammie sighs and walks over to the closet. She opens it noisily, and I see a neat row of tiny clothes arranged on hangers. Sailor suits; blue, white, yellow and green jumpers; a little red coat for the cold weather. There are three pairs of shoes on the floor, baby shoes, soft leather, and a sled propped up in the corner.

"They had kids?"

"One," Grammie finally shares. "A baby boy. He died."

For some reason, I feel like I've been kicked in the stomach. I mean, it actually hurts, being in this room, this dead baby's room. Grammie smiles weakly and looks like she might feel a little sick herself. "They didn't change a thing. Just left it like this all these years. I can't believe it. I'd heard the rumours but…" She shakes her head and gazes around, the afternoon light through the ancient blind over the window mellowing and softening everything in the room. The white dresser with the teddy on top, the rocking horse, the crib, the chair, the changing table, the braided oval rug on the bare floor. Eerie. But not just that. It's so sad that I want to cry. A lump comes up in my throat, and I need to swallow hard a few times to force it back down.

Grammie eases herself into the rocking chair by the window. She feels more comfortable here, like she belongs. I don't want to sit down. I want to leave, but I can tell Grammie's not ready—and if Grammie's not ready, it ain't gonna happen. So I ask, "Did you ever see the baby? I mean, when you were a kid?"

She shakes her head, staring at the red fire engine she's taken from the wide, low windowsill. It isn't plastic like most of the toys nowadays, and I can hear the clank of metal as Grammie turns it round to examine it. "No," she answers but still doesn't look up. I think about sitting cross-legged on that rug in the centre of the room but change my mind and instead go to lean in the doorway.

"I saw her in town a couple of times when she was pregnant." Grammie looks at me now, and I can see that her eyes are wet and her nose is getting redder by the minute. "She was so happy. Euphoric, in fact, bubbling on about her plans for the baby, about names, about this nursery, about being a mother. One time, when we met on main street, she told me that she hoped her baby would turn out as good and as sweet as I did. That's exactly how she put it. 'As good and as sweet.' Imagine that!

"My father said she was the same way with him later on, when she was getting close to being due, and he'd deliver their groceries. She'd talk to him all day, if he'd let her." She chuckles softly, remembering. "Katherine was so nervous about being a mother. She told me that she'd convinced her husband, Thomas, to let her buy several baby books so that she could read up on what she should expect. That one loved to study! She was always reading something, trying to figure things out. Some people can accept things the way they are, just let it go, so to speak. Not Katherine. It didn't seem she could rest until she had the answers, had things solved. I loved that about her."

Grammie sighs and turns around awkwardly, setting the toy back up on the sill in front of the closed blind.

"So what happened? To the baby." I almost hate to ask but feel like I might burst if I don't find out.

"Well, one of those times Thomas was away in Halifax…" Grammie pauses to push herself out of the rocker, "…Robert, that was his name, died in his sleep. Crib death perhaps, or maybe he was sick with the flu, and Katherine couldn't bring the fever down. I don't know for sure." She shrugs. "I only ever heard the stories, like everyone else."

"That's terrible! I mean, she was alone here, and her baby *died*? That's…it's just not *right*. It's not fair." Even to myself, I sound like a little kid. Nothing's fair, but Grammie agrees anyway.

"No. It's not fair." I get out of the way, and she steps past me into the hallway. "Not fair at all that so much tragedy can take place in one household. But it did, and does, all the time. That's just the way it goes sometimes." I turn to follow, closing the nursery door behind me and feeling a chill as I do.

"What do you suppose is in here?" It's clear to me now that Grammie's got her mind set on looking in every room. The next door on our right, across the hall and next door to the bathroom, is shut but not quite latched. Grammie pushes on it, and it reluctantly swings open wide. "Looks like this must've been his study."

I think she's right. There's a huge desk with a wooden swivel chair positioned behind it under the window along the east wall. "Look at that fireplace! Cool! It's almost as big as the one downstairs!" I say.

Grammie clucks her tongue. By now she's in the room and once again has her hands on everything. She's got me wanting to feel the stuff in here, too. Plus, this room has a better feeling than the baby's room, and it's not a bathroom, so I don't mind the idea of touching things in here. I reach out and lay my hand flat on the broad surface of Thomas O'Leary's desk, right next to the faded green rectangular thing in its centre. "Grammie? What's this?" I pick it up in a thin cloud of dust, and it leaves a perfectly clean spot on the desktop.

She comes over to me from where she was examining the ceiling-high bookcase across the room by the fireplace. "It's an ink blotter, to soak up any splotches of ink that he might've spilled or that dripped from his pen." I lay it back down, and Grammie walks over to one of the two windows on the south wall that looks out over the strait. This room has the same carpet as the hallway, and her feet don't make any sound at all. It's like she's floating over the floor. Grammie tugs gently at the bottom of a yellowed blind, holding the bottom so that it can roll up slowly. I do the same thing at the tall window next to it, the one closest to the fireplace. Below us is a huge yard smothered by long, ragged grass and tall weeds, all browning from the frosty nights. Beyond that is the strait, points of light hard and shining like diamonds, a blue darker than the sky, and deeper.

"Nice view," I comment, squinting against the brightness, my eyes having gotten used to the dark in the house.

"Mmmm," Grammie nods. "Sure is. Kept the nicest room for himself."

I guess it's true. This room has a fireplace all its own and is the biggest by far of the upstairs rooms. It's obviously not Katherine's study. I mean, it looks like a guy's space. There's a painting of hunting dogs on the wall beside his desk and a wide leather chair in front of the fireplace partly covered with a white sheet. The books in the case that shares a wall with the bathroom look thick and imposing. It's all business in here.

Grammie must've been noticing the same kind of stuff, because she says, "This even smells like a man's room, doesn't it?" As soon as she says it, we both breathe in deep.

"What is that?" There's something about the smell in here that I don't recognize.

"I'm not sure." She sniffs the air and I think of those hunting dogs, two hounds, with their noses pointed towards their prey. "Pipe smoke! I bet that's what it is! Gets into the carpet, the furniture, everything. Shortly after your Grampie and I got married, he thought it'd be a good idea to take up smoking a pipe. That didn't last long. I told him he had a choice: he could have me in the house or that thing." She laughs. "Fortunately, he chose me."

I pull down my shade and Grammie does the same. There's one more room nearest the end of the hall yet to see. I lead the way towards it, this door closed, too. I feel the cool of the glass knob and recall that Grammie has one like it on her front door. It doesn't screech when I turn it, and the door doesn't creak as it opens. The master bedroom. Makes sense. They had to sleep somewhere, and we haven't seen a bedroom yet.

Knowing how to do it now without making a racket, I walk over to the window on the east wall and ease up the shade. It doesn't want to roll up as easily as the one in the study and, in the end, I only coax it halfway open. But it's enough. Now the light can come in through the dense lace curtain. To the right of this window is a tall bureau with four deep drawers and a dust-laden top. The sheet that used to cover it lies on the floor around its base.

Grammie's on the other side of room, admiring a low dressing table with a huge, round mirror. What catches my eye is an old trunk sitting at the foot of Katherine's bed. It's pretty beaten up. I touch it, and under my hand it feels like leather, sturdy and smooth. I wonder what all the stamps on it are for.

"Grammie." She turns away from the dresser to look at me. The second she does, I see Katherine in that dusty mirror. She's not making eye contact with me. Doesn't even seem to know I'm there. Her reflection is sitting at the table on that stool tucked beneath it, and she's brushing out her long hair. In her hand, Grammie holds the brush Katherine's reflection is running through her hair. Then the image is gone.

"Charly! What is it? You're pale as a ghost!"

I point stupidly at the dressing table mirror. "Did you see her?"

"See who? Katherine? Where?" Grammie whirls

around to face the direction in which I'm pointing and asks again, "Where?"

Slowly I lower my arm. "She's gone."

"Where did you see her?" There's an impatient edge to Grammie's question, the spaces between her words deliberate.

"In the mirror. Not really her. Just her reflection. And only for a second." I let go of the breath I've been holding and tell her, "Look. I wanna go now."

Grammie touches my arm. "Okay…" Her eyes stop on something right behind me, and her hand drops from my arm. She's still holding the hairbrush with its long, gold handle. "That wasn't there before, was it?"

I turn to see what she's talking about. There's a yellow and blue hatbox sitting on top of the trunk I'd just been looking at. Beside it, lying on the worn leather, a note. Grammie reaches down, glances at the words on the stationery, then hands it quickly to me.

"Looks like it's for you."

The hat is for Charly.
With fondness,
Katherine O'Leary

"Let's go home, girl." Grammie sighs heavily and shakes her head. "I've had enough excitement for one day."

Six

In her narrow driveway alongside the house, Grammie takes her car out of gear and shuts off the engine. On the way home from Katherine's (not a long drive—maybe five minutes), I told her most everything about the morning before: the change in the O'Leary house from old to new, my visit with Katherine, the fact I'd only been gone from our house for a few minutes.

Grammie didn't look at me or say much. She just watched the road, nodding and making those "mmm" sounds to show me she was interested and actually listening. Now, still in the car, she turns towards me.

"That must've been some visit." That's just like Grammie, holding out. She doesn't tell me whether she believes me or not, and that's what I want to know. She has to. She saw the hatbox, knew it hadn't been there before. And she did see the note. There's no faking something like that.

I'd been wanting to ask for hours now, but didn't know how to pose the question. Before I can form the words in my mind, it slips out and into the air between us. "How'd she die?"

Grammie eases back into her seat, and it's obvious we're not getting out of the car quite yet. She lifts her shoulders a little and, for some unknown reason, adjusts her side mirror as if the answer might show up behind her, closer than it appears. "No one's really certain."

"You've talked about rumours. There must be some about Katherine's death." I wait, but she doesn't answer until I nearly beg. "I want to know."

"The rumour accepted by most folks is that her husband drowned her in the well out back—or maybe he hired someone else to do it. I don't think, though, that you can pin murder on a man because of his mean looks and nasty disposition. It takes more than ugly in a bad mood to commit murder. There're some that speculate that he may've sent her off to an asylum in Ontario after their boy died." Grammie sighs. "She wasn't the same after that. Nobody saw her much. She didn't come out of their house and go downtown or to church like she used to. I remember that people thought she'd snap out of it eventually, but she never did. In the end, she fell out of touch with everyone she'd known."

"What do you think?" I turn so that my knee is resting on the seat and nudging the armrest that separates us.

"I don't know. I've always hoped that she left. Went back to Halifax or somewhere, anywhere, and started a new life." She laughs, kind of sadly. "When I was young, I would make up little stories about her in my mind, how she'd robbed her husband to get enough money to put herself through teacher's college. Then I pictured her teaching in a one-room schoolhouse out west and marrying a handsome rancher who knew nothing of her past and didn't want to." Grammie's eyes are serious. "All we can know is that Katherine disappeared. Probably, the ending wasn't happy at all. That's why you were able to visit her. Contentedly dead people aren't known to hang around much. Usually, they've got somewhere else to go."

There's my answer! She believes me. Yes!

Inside the back door, Grammie calls out, "We're home!" Nobody answers. We take off our shoes and coats and head on into the kitchen. There's a note from Mom on the island, a pen laid across it diagonally.

Mom and Charly,
Took Nikki for lunch at the harbour. We'll be back for supper.
XXX OOO
Sylvia/Mom

"I'm glad your mom's doing something with that girl. She's so mopey. They both are. Maybe this'll be good for them." Grammie reaches up into the cupboard above the microwave and brings down the electric kettle. "Want some hot chocolate?"

It's true. They've both been slouching around since we got here, but I gotta admit that I haven't exactly been president of the Glee Club myself lately. "Yeah, sure."

Grammie turns around, her eyes level on me, her hand on the kettle cord, ready to plug it in. Her way of reminding me.

"Please."

She smiles and fits the plug into the outlet by the sink. Pulling up a stool, she perches next to me, turned so that we're facing each other. It feels a little too close, and I shift my butt on the seat. Oh, no. I recognize that look. Grammie's got me alone in the house and wants to *talk*. Not friendly chatter over a deck of cards, but that dragging-it-all-out-in-the-open-post-parental-divorce-type talk. In short, no fun. Frankly, I'd rather stick a pin in my eye. She takes a deep breath. I hold my ground and brace myself. Here it comes.

"How about you, Charly?"

Great. A question. Requiring an answer from me. Nice opening.

"I think the kettle's boiling." I try to slide down from my stool, but with lightning speed and strength that should be impossible in a woman her age, Grammie grasps my knee with a look that says, "Oh no, you don't." She stares straight into my eyes.

Her voice deceivingly sweet, she reminds me, "You know that old kettle. It takes forever to boil." She waves her free hand, the one not clamped on me like a steel trap, in a dismissive way. "So you just relax and let me worry about the hot chocolate."

There's a long pause, during which her eyes bore into me. There's no way out, so I talk. "What about me?"

"You know what I mean. Your mom and Nikki are obviously taking some time to adjust. And Lord knows, it's a tough adjustment. But you're harder to read. More like your dad that way, I think. You can hide the way you feel and wear a pretty good mask." She leans forward, even closer, but at least her hand's finally off my knee. "I want to know how you're really doing."

I shrug. "Fine, I guess."

"You feel left out with your mom and Nikki going into Charlottetown for lunch?"

"Not really." Which is true, because it's nice not to have them around for a while. They're both so, I don't know, cold. Moody, too. It's like you've got to tiptoe around them, never knowing what you'll do to set them stomping off.

"Why not? You didn't want to go with them?"

"Not really." It was fine going exploring with Grammie and telling her about Katherine (and she actually believes me!). Plus, if they went to Charlottetown, they'll eat in some tearoom in a shop and afterwards wander around looking at antiques and tablecloths and greeting cards. Then they'll go from store window to store window downtown and peer into every one like it was a crystal ball, and they were desperate to see the future. I would've died of boredom. No, this is definitely better.

"You miss your dad?" Now the kettle is boiling for real, and Grammie hops down from her chair to unplug it.

"I guess." Grammie stands on her plastic stepping stool to reach the fancier pottery mugs she keeps on the top shelf of the cupboard nearest the fridge. I can understand why she goes to the trouble. I like them too. Cool and smooth on the outside, with those perfectly spaced ridges on the inside, a new one appearing each time you take a drink. That's something I wouldn't mind doing, making pottery. "I'll see him at Christmas."

Standing on the other side of the island, Grammie dumps heaping teaspoonfuls of chocolate powder into the chosen mugs then adds the water still boiling, so that it goes "blurp-blurp" as she pours it. "That's a ways off, still. Long time not to see a parent. Or your friends." She pushes my drink towards me and warns, "Wait for it to cool down a bit."

"Thanks. I will." I blow on it. I do miss Allie. When we'd first arrived here, I'd written her a couple of long letters, telling her about this place, saying that maybe next year, I'd come home and live with Dad. Then she and I could hang out again. I got one card from her with a picture of a cat on it. Not a cartoon cat, not something funny, just a photograph of a cat curled up sleeping. Inside it said: "You're purrr-fect." She'd written something like: *Hi Charly! How are you! School's great this year! I'm playing volleyball! Love ya! Allie.* I didn't write back after that. Dad's called once since we've been at Grammie's. Truth is, I'm not sure if we're going home for Christmas or not. "I miss Allie, but I don't know if she misses me." I try to sip my hot chocolate. Way too hot. Grammie wriggles back up onto the stool beside me.

"Why do you say that?"

I shrug. "I dunno. Haven't heard from her—well, once. But she didn't say much."

"Hmm." Grammie hasn't tried her hot chocolate yet. "You know, Charly, for you, life has changed a lot. New house, new school, new town on the other side of the country. It's kind of a different family, too, isn't it? With me here all the time and your dad gone." Her voice goes softer, and she's not right in my face any more. "For your friend, life hasn't changed that much. She's only thinking about what's happening right now for her. You might still be remembering how things were. Sort of caught between two worlds. You'll settle in, though. You already are. The way you're exploring around, getting to know the place, taking an interest, doing well in school." She pauses and touches her mug before adding, "Don't tell them, but I think you're doing better than either your mom or Nikki. I think you're just more resilient, in some ways. They'll catch up to you, soon enough." It's her turn to shrug. "Or maybe they never will."

Now she takes a drink, and I do the same. It's warm and sweet and good. Sometimes Grammie can be a pain, but other times, she knows exactly what to say.

Seven

"Hey! Wait up!" I turn around and squint into the sun at Derek running to catch up to me after school. He's holding his backpack by the loop on its top. It looks heavy and makes him run kinda lopsided. The wind blows his hair into his eyes. As he reaches me, he tosses his head to one side, and an errant shock of red follows the motion.

"Hey. How's it going? Haven't seen you around much," I say. It's true. I've hardly seen my cousin since the day we broke into Katherine's place with Nikki and Mark. You'd never know we go to the same school.

He steps up beside me. "Yeah. That's cause I've been avoidin' you. Nah. Just kiddin', Char." He pats me on the back as if we've just played a hockey game and won. "How you like livin' over at Grammie's?"

"It's good." I slide my backpack off my shoulder and hold it by its loop like my cousin's doing. This way, there's something between us to help prevent any more unwanted physical contact.

"Grammie's funny, isn't she? She cracks me up. But she drives Mom crazy. That's why we don't come over a

58

whole bunch. They like each other all right, but like Mom says, for short periods of time."

"My mom and Grammie get along pretty good, but you can tell they're mother and daughter." I want to add that they sometimes treat each other like Nikki and Mom treat each other, but I keep it to myself.

"Yeah. Girls. Guess they never change even after they grow up."

Out the corner of my eye, I see Derek grinning, waiting for me to react. He doesn't have to wait long.

"At least they grow up."

He stops dead in his tracks. "Ouch!" But instead of sounding mad, he sounds kind of impressed or something. He only pauses for a beat, then falls back in step beside me. Now we feel equal. "Hey, that was weird over at the old O'Leary house the other day, wasn't it?"

My heart speeds up. Truth is, I was trying to think of a way to bring that day up. That my cousin beat me to it catches me off guard. "Uhh...what was weird?" Let's see what he'll say to that.

"You know..." He hesitates, glances over at me. "In the room..."

I help him out, give him some hope that maybe I know what he's talking about. "In the parlour?"

"No. In the living room place."

"It's the same place. 'Parlour' is an old-fashioned word for living room. They're pretty much the same thing."

"Since when'd you become a historian?"

"Since when did you learn four-syllable words?" This

time, I can tell he's had enough. He doesn't smile, and instead his mouth forms a hard, straight line. Instantly I regret being so sarcastic. I really don't mind Derek, and I like that he wants to talk about Katherine's house. I don't know what my problem is. "Sorry," I say.

He shrugs and doesn't say anything, so I keep talking. After all, I do want to know if he remembers what happened there in Katherine's house as I remember it. "Yeah, it was weird, what happened. Scared me, that's for sure. You must've been a little scared too. You ran out of there as fast as I did."

This gets him to speak, but only to push me further into my side of the story. "What made you run?"

Cornered. "Oh, you know...you were there. I'm sure you saw it too."

"Saw what?" He's just not gonna let me off the hook.

We stop walking and face one another there on the sidewalk, a yellow leaf drifting down between us from the baring branches above. I take a deep breath. So much for me making Derek admit first that he saw something. Here goes. "When we were on the couch, it felt and looked like someone sat down between us. The cushions moved, they sank in." Derek stares at me incredulously, and I feel my conviction slip away. "Unless it was my imagination..." I hate the way my words trail off pathetically.

My cousin's expression changes, softens. "Naw. It wasn't your imagination, Char, unless it was mine, too." Derek to the rescue. "It even *felt* like someone was right there. Scared the crap outta me."

60

All I can say is "Thanks."

"For what?"

I lift my shoulders and smile at him. "For being scared, too, but mostly for admitting it." We're gonna get along just fine.

He looks past me, squinting into the sky in the direction of downtown. "Anyway, Grammie's invited us to dinner tonight. Since we're walking that way, maybe I'll just come over now and give Mom a call from your place."

"Sounds good. Grammie'll make us some of her hot chocolate, and Nikki will ignore us."

At the kitchen table, Grammie sets the anticipated mugs of hot chocolate in front of my cousin and me. She doesn't join us but works at the sink, "fussing" she calls it, because there's really not much left to do. I can smell the chicken and vegetables roasting in the oven. On the island sits a big basket of her homemade buns, a couple of two-litre bottles of pop and a store-bought pecan pie. I'm hungry, but the hot chocolate will help me wait.

"Smells good in here, Grammie," Derek comments after trying to take a drink of his too-hot beverage. "When do we eat?"

"When your folks get here. Try not to gnaw your own arm off in the meantime." Grammie passes behind him on the way out to the sun porch and ruffles his hair.

When she's out of the room, he leans towards me. "Did you tell Grammie about the O'Leary house? She believes in ghosts, you know. And she also knows all the stories. I heard most of them from her. Has she taken you on 'the tour'?"

I chuckle and test my hot chocolate with my tongue. Perfect. "Yeah. She did. Kinda freaky."

"Not really. I don't believe most of it..."

"Most of what?" Grammie's standing right behind my cousin, the huge punchbowl she'd retrieved from the porch in her hands.

I answer for him, "He doesn't believe most of the stories from around here. We were talking about the tour." Ow. Derek nudges my leg with his foot a bit too hard, but it's too late to stop it. The wrath of Grammie falls upon him. Very coolly, very slowly, she walks over to the island and sets down the large glass bowl. Then she turns deliberately to look at my cousin. He's avoiding her eyes and sipping wildly at his hot chocolate, as if drinking it uses all his concentration.

I'm surprised when she doesn't say anything but instead disappears into the living room. I whisper to Derek, "Where's she going?" and he whispers back, "You'll see." I get the impression he's been through this before. In an instant Grammie reappears with both our coats, one in each hand.

"What?" I stammer. "Where are we going?" How I got involved in this apparent dispute is what I want to know.

"It's still light out for an hour or so. Put your coats on, and I'll drive you both out to the woods. You can go for a nice walk before dinner." Grammie's tone adamant.

Is she serious? I'm not going anywhere near those woods, no matter how farfetched the stories. Nothing's worth taking that kind of chance. It's creepy around there. It seems that Derek agrees.

"Okay, okay, Grammie." He sighs heavily. "I believe in the stories. You know I do. I just didn't want to scare Charly." He winks at me, but I don't think Grammie sees.

She doesn't believe him for a second. I can tell by the way she says flatly, "What a gentleman." She turns then, and I can hear the faint sound of coat hangers moving against each other as she hangs our coats back up. I've learned a lesson here tonight, and it'll be a long time (if ever) before I tell Grammie I don't believe her stories.

I want to be diplomatic and smooth things over between Grammie and Derek, so I ask, "Grammie, did I tell you what happened to Derek and me when we went to Katherine's house with Mark and Nikki that day?"

She looks up from the punchbowl into which she's pouring the last of the pop. "No." I've obviously caught her interest, because, before I can continue, she grabs her half-finished cup of tea and sits down at the table with us. "So what happened to you two?" Grammie looks at one then the other of us, impatiently awaiting an answer. She really does love this stuff!

Derek looks at me, and I read in his expression, raised eyebrows and all, that he wants me to start. "Well, Derek and me were in the parlour—you and I never got that far." Then to Derek, "Grammie and I just explored upstairs." Back to Grammie, "We were looking at the books and stuff, then we both sat down on the couch, Derek on one end, me on the other. Anyway, we're sitting there, and all of a sudden it feels like someone sits down between us."

"We could feel their weight on the cushions, see the

depression that they were making," Derek breaks in.

"Really?" There's wonder in Grammie's voice. She leans back in her chair and takes a big gulp of tea before looking at us both and asking, "What did you do?"

Together, we answer, "We ran!"

"And that's not all. Remember when we were walking away, back towards the school?"

Derek nods and answers, "'Course I remember. A baby crying."

"Loud."

"Real loud." Derek pushes up his glasses and pushes away his empty mug.

Automatically, Grammie stands up and takes her mug along with Derek's to the dishwasher. She opens it and pauses, both mugs still in hand. "Let me get this straight. You both ran because you both felt someone sit down beside you, then outside you both heard the baby crying?"

Derek and I nod at each other, then at Grammie.

"Wow. She does like you, Charly. I've ridden my bike down the road past the house, cut flowers from the yard in the summer and walked the shoreline where it lies, and until I went there with you, I never heard or saw anything unusual."

Now Derek speaks up. "Me, neither. I been there a few times—not inside—but around, like you—" nods in Grammie's direction "—and nothing weird ever happened. It wasn't even that spooky from the outside."

He studies me long enough to make me feel uncomfortable, until Grammie says, "Did she tell you the ghost left her a sun hat?"

She walks back over to the table, lays a hand on my shoulder and comments, "Looks like we have a regular little ghost magnet living under my roof." She pats me, adding, "Things could get interesting around here."

The doorbell rings, and Derek leaps up. "That's Mom and Dad. I'll get it."

Saved by the bell.

Eight

It's been a week, and here I am again. I left Grammie in the car playing her Gameboy and listening to the radio. I told her I wanted to go alone this time.

"I have to see if it'll happen again—if the house will change, if Katherine will be there."

"Okay." I expected more of an argument from her but she only said, "If you're not back in half-an-hour, I'm coming in there after you."

"It's a deal."

I'm standing at the front door in the shade and wearing the floppy sun hat that Katherine gave to me. It isn't my style, but I don't want to hurt her feelings. It all happened again. As I stepped through the old gate and into Katherine's yard, the house seemed to straighten up and become a brighter white. The grass got greener and shorter. Those crumbled and busted stones were complete again and made a neat path right up to her front stoop. That's where I am now, the porch swing hanging motionless to my left, down where the veranda turns a corner. I'm stuck here at the door deciding whether or not to knock. Hesitating, I glance over my shoulder to see that both Grammie and her car are gone. My head snaps back around when suddenly the door is flung open wide.

"Charly! Good to see you!"

"Hi." The word pops out of my mouth propelled by my thudding heart, and I feel like I've got to catch my breath. Katherine looks more casual today, but still dressed up. Her hair's covered with a bright orange scarf, and instead of a skirt, she wears snug-fitting tan pants that end about halfway between her ankles and her knees.

"What a surprise. Come on in." She does seem surprised to see me appear on her doorstep. Almost as surprised as I must have looked when she opened her front door. She steps aside and gestures for me to walk in past her. As I do, the smell of the house hits me. Gone is the musty abandoned air that invaded my nostrils when I was here with Grammie. Instead, I detect freshly baked bread and lemon polish. Once again, the banister is dustless, the carpet a clean red, and the rooms flooded with light.

Inside the entrance, I take off the hat and clutch it in my hands. Katherine motions toward it with her left hand. Her fingernails are painted bright pink, and I notice for the first time her gold wedding band. "I see you got the hat."

"Yes. Thanks. It sure is…" I falter, searching wildly for the right word, "big." Not the word I was going for.

She laughs. "At any rate, it'll keep the sun off you when you're out and about. Plus, it looks cute on you, but then, what wouldn't? I was just about to head outside myself. You want some lemonade?"

"If you're busy, I can come over another…"

"No." For a moment, her voice loses those fluffy edges and becomes hard, kind of desperate-sounding, but it lightens right back up again. "Stay. We can visit outside, and I'll show you my flowers."

"Sure." Then I tack on, "Sounds good." All of a sudden, I'm feeling a bit like I've got to reassure her. Think about it. Me, having to reassure a ghost. If anything, it should be the other way around.

In the kitchen, bright and scrubbed to shining (unlike Grammie's kitchen), Katherine pours lemonade into two tall glasses and puts the glass jug back in the squat fridge with its rounded corners. "Hope it's sweet enough for you. Try it."

I take a sip and it's cold, way colder than I expect. And perfect. It tastes like maybe there's even a real lemon in it. Nothing powdered or packaged about this stuff. I gulp down half a glass standing there. When I come up for air, I tell my host, "It's good."

She smiles and walks back to the fridge. "I can see that. Here." She tops up my glass from a jug that doesn't seem to get any emptier, and we head back out to the veranda. From Katherine's front porch, there's still no sign of Grammie or of the paved road, even. It's dirt now, and narrower, running closer to Katherine's gate. The sky's high and clear, those clouds that hovered low over us on the way here now gone. For a second, I wonder if I'll ever get back to where I belong, but then

Katherine's speaking, and I pay attention. Like Grammie says, I'll cross that bridge when I come to it.

"My begonias are doing well this year." At the base of the stairs coming up to the veranda there're two square, wooden planters I've never seen before painted crisp white and loaded with bright red fat flowers. "They like a lot of water." Katherine reaches down into one of the boxes and pulls off a dead leaf.

"Pretty." I don't usually talk much about flowers, but this seems to be a fairly appropriate comment. What else is there to say? They *are* pretty.

"Let's head around back. I've got a lot more to show you."

We step out of the shade, and now I'm glad for this shapeless straw hat with its thick yellow ribbon around the crown. The sun is hot! We walk on the lawn around the east side of the house in the direction of that narrow dirt road, where there's still no sight of Grammie or the car. Only someone's old horse grazing in a pasture on the other side of the road near a falling-down old barn, boards weathered grey. None of these things exist any more, and yet I'm here. So while I'm here, do I exist? I don't want to think about it too much.

"This is my garden. I planted it here right near the kitchen door so I can run out and get whatever I need close at hand." Katherine leads me past the kitchen door and a set of stairs leading up to it, small and not as straight as the ones out in front.

Her garden is huge. Grammie told me she usually has one, but the plot isn't this big. This past year,

Grammie said she was too busy volunteering with the library's summer program to have a garden, so the red dirt rectangle stayed neatly tilled up. Mr. MacFee from next door takes care of that.

"What are these?" I bend down, trying not to spill my lemonade, and brush the tips of a bunch of waxy leaves, deep red veins trekking across each of them.

"Beets."

"And those?" I point to the next long, straight row over, a tall stake marking either end.

Katherine looks at me. She hasn't drunk much of her lemonade. "You don't work in the garden much, do you?"

"It's that obvious?"

"They're potatoes."

"Oh." Here I am in potatoland, and I don't even know what potato plants look like. I try to explain. "I've only seen them out in the fields, or in other people's gardens back home. I've never really seen one up close."

Katherine just smiles, a smile that tells me she feels mildly sorry for me, robbed in my youth of extensive plant knowledge and gardening experience. I get my vegetables where everyone else does: the grocery store. Works for me.

As we move along the edge, she continues to educate me, telling me the names of the vegetables in the rows, tapping the top of each marker as she goes. I'm not really paying attention, just smiling and nodding and wondering how she died and why she's still here, sipping lemonade and showing me her garden. And how come it's so warm in this place at the end of

October, anyway? Nobody has a full garden or blooming flowers this late, so what's up?

Our garden tour brings us to the back of the house looking down the sloping yard to where it ends at the sea grasses, sharp-looking as razors and springing up out of the coarse sand. The sun off the strait is blinding, and I have to look away and blink, yellow and blue shadows chasing each other behind my eyes when I do.

"I love this view." Katherine's shielding her eyes with her left hand.

"Yeah. It's something. Nothing like this back home, that's for sure." It's true. There's nothing like this on the prairies. No river even comes close, and you can't really compare this scene to any lake view.

She keeps talking as if she doesn't hear me. "Makes staying here seem almost bearable."

Then I spot something over to my right that makes my mouth go dry and my palms sweat. Painted that same sparkling white and sitting about the middle of the backyard is the well. In her flat black shoes, Katherine strides across the lawn, pausing to set her half-full glass on the wide arm of one of two lawn chairs, neither of which I've ever seen. I set my empty glass down on the other chair and follow her. At the edge of the well, she stops, the peaked roof over it shading only her face. She lifts off the wooden cover, leaning it up against the well's enclosure.

Then Katherine leans over slightly, and my breath catches in my throat. I imagine I can hear her screams as she's thrown in and the lid is replaced, her voice in the deep blue night echoing off the red cliffs until she can't tread water any more. Then it's quiet.

"Good," she comments and I step up beside her, leaning further over the well because, frankly, I'm a lot shorter. "The water level's up."

A long way down, I can just make out the shimmering reflection of daylight. If she drowned there, she doesn't remember.

"Looks deep." Stupid, I know. Of course it's deep. It's a well. But Katherine just grins, stands back up straight, and the sunlight falls again on her face as she bends to grab the well cover. She replaces it with a dull thunk. The air out here is salty, so salty that I can nearly taste it on my lips.

"Let's sit down for a bit, enjoy the sun." She sees my empty glass as we approach those chairs. "Want some more? Or are you okay?"

"I'm fine—thanks." Katherine's got a flowerbed that runs the length of the back of the house. It's full of flowers, oranges, purples, yellows and a lot of blue bunches. I sit down and way back in the deep chair so that my feet don't quite touch the ground. Katherine sits with her legs crossed and looks out over the strait, down the shoreline. It's cooler back here because of the breeze coming off the water. "What month is it, anyway?"

"August, of course." I feel her glance at me for a second then turn her eyes back to the water and take another sip of her lemonade.

I keep going. "At my house, it's October. And cold. No more gardens, no more flowers. Might snow tomorrow."

"Where do you live?" She sounds confused.

"In town."

"Oh." Katherine thinks a moment, then adds, "That's strange."

I agree. "Yup. Sure is. Time is different at your house. Everything's different. Newer, or something."

"Newer?"

"Yeah," I don't know where to go from here, but I plow on, trying to explain how I see things so she'll know. "From town, your house looks old. You know. No paint, no porch swing, a rusty gate and falling-down fence. Like it's all been here a long time with no one living in it, looking after it." I swallow hard. Now I want that lemonade.

Katherine sighs but still doesn't look at me. "So I've been here that long, have I?"

I shrug. "I dunno. I guess." Then I ask her, "Why are you here? Aren't you dead?"

This time, she looks right at me. "Pardon me?" She says this like a mother or a teacher.

"Uhhh…well, aren't you, like, a ghost?"

Katherine laughs and shakes her head at me. "You sure are a forward little thing, aren't you?"

My face goes hot. "Sorry. I just…it's the only explanation." Then I burst out, "You've just gotta be a ghost! This whole place is a ghost! Because I've *seen* it all broken down and old—the way it really is."

"Are you saying that my house isn't real? That I'm not real?" Katherine cocks her head to the side and looks at me hard. When she does this, I can't tell if she's admonishing me or if she's just kidding. She lays a hand on her bare arm and runs it up and down. "I sure feel real." Katherine brings the palm of her hand down hard on the wide armrest. "And everything around me feels pretty real. How do you explain that, girl?"

"I…I'm not sure."

She laughs again, finishes her lemonade in one gulp and admits, "I have to say I can't explain it either, but I think you're right, Charly. I think I *am* a ghost." As she says this, she keeps staring out over the strait, squinting against the glare of light shifting on water. "Time is strange here, you know? That's my biggest hint. It doesn't move in a straight line any more. Often, it seems to slide sideways so that summer veers off somehow into early spring, then, a week later, it might be the dead of winter." Katherine gestures towards the sky with her right hand. "And sunrise, sunset, I never know when they're going to happen, whereas I used to measure my life by their predictability. Days would come and go and, as each one did, I'd get a little older." She shrugs and turns her head to face me. "Now, I stay the same. I might've been like this for years or months or days. I can't tell. I can't depend on time any more, and I don't know how, but somehow I must exist outside of it."

She exists outside of time. When I'm here, maybe I'm outside of time, too. That would explain a lot.

"You wanna walk up to the capes?" I ask.

A piece of hair escapes from her orange scarf and blows across Katherine's forehead. She brushes it away with the back of her hand. "Can't."

"Why not?" I move forward and sit up straight so

that my feet are flat on the ground in front of me.

She lifts her hands to show she feels helpless and tells me, "I just can't. I've never been able to leave here. I think I'm scared. The fear's as solid as a wall, and I can't get past it." She indicates the well and past the lawn to where the sea grasses cut through the red sand. "I get there, to where the yard ends, and I just start to shake from head to toe until I can barely stand up. My heart pounds so hard it hurts, and I sweat all over. For me, there's no getting away. Something's holding me back. I don't think I can beat it, Charly. That's just how it is." Katherine sighs and stands up, leaving her glass behind as she strolls out across the lawn in the direction of the capes.

I follow, and when we get near to the edge of the lawn before it turns untamed, Katherine stops. She holds out her hands, reaching towards the shore. The colour washes out of her face, even though she's obviously wearing as much make-up as Nikki does when she's out the door to see a boyfriend.

As always, it's my left hand that reacts first. I reach out, imitating Katherine, and don't feel a thing. Only the cool salt breeze on my open palms, but I can see Katherine's hands shake. She looks terrified, her mouth drawn in a tight, straight line, her green eyes wide, stuck open.

Without thinking, I draw in a deep breath and lunge forward off the neat lawn and into the sand and sea grass. I hear Katherine's gasp, but I keep going. I've walked along this shore a lot, but from here it looks different. A lot wider. And there seems to be many more sandbars, dark and flat places in the shallow sparkling water. On down the beach those capes look taller, redder in the summer sun.

Without thinking, I come back and take Katherine's wrist in my hand. She kind of jumps. "Sorry," I say, but I don't let go, just keep holding on gently and feeling the trembling there beneath her skin, through her bones. We stand like that on the edge of her yard looking out over the water for awhile. I don't look at Katherine, just watch the swooping gulls and listen to the waves. It's as if I can *feel* her calm down beside me. Finally, I ask the question I've been wanting to.

"Why don't you try to come with me?"

Nine

Katherine doesn't answer me, and I don't let go of her wrist. Instead, I start to move slowly, bit by bit, taking baby steps in the direction of the shore. She seems to want to try it, even though she's scared. I know that feeling. It's like when I wanted to take guitar lessons. I was terrified that I'd be awful and that my teacher would tell me so. Still, I worked up the courage and asked Mom to sign me up for lessons at the music store.

That night, I was so nervous, I couldn't even hold down the strings. But Evan (my teacher) was really nice—and cute!—and he just sort of showed me around the blue electric guitar. He told me the names of the strings, showed me how to plug it into the amplifier and told me what the four knobs on its body were for. The next week, I was way less nervous and even looking forward to the lesson a bit. I was going to learn the C-major scale. The week after that, Mom took us to live here with Grammie on Prince Edward Island.

"I can't believe it…" I can barely hear Katherine's words. "I'm here." She means outside of her yard. It takes us probably about ten minutes to get off the lawn and down the sand bank leading to the shore. My friend begins to move forward on her own, and I finally let go of her wrist. "It looks so different out here than it does from my yard."

"Yeah. I noticed that, too." There're more gulls over here, that's for sure. Some screech and sweep down low, their wing tips grazing the water, while others soar along soundlessly, lazily letting the sea breeze carry them, their bodies moving white spots against the water and sky. North of the shore a ways, there are rich, red potato fields.

Without another word, Katherine suddenly dashes down to the shoreline, her flat shoes slapping and leaving their prints in the wet sand closest to the water's edge. As I half-run after her, sand gets in my shoes, and I can feel it shift and bunch and spread out again. I plunk down on a weather-worn log, smooth and bleached white, taking off my shoes first, tipping them so the sand runs out, then peeling off my socks.

"Good idea," Katherine agrees and flops down beside me, her cheeks flushed and her breath coming quick. She takes off her shoes too, and she's not wearing socks. We leave our shoes there by the log and sprint towards the strait.

Katherine doesn't hesitate at the shallow water licking away at the sand, but instead leaps right in, her steps causing a series of quick splashes, as she runs in the shallows west towards the capes. Me, I don't like the sudden shock of the cold ocean but can't resist putting in my bare feet just the same. So I do, but when I run after her, I stay mostly on the sand or, when I can reach them without getting my feet wetter than necessary, I jump from sandbar to sandbar. Not far ahead of me, I see Katherine doing the same thing, only with lots of splashing. She kinda looks like she's dancing, her arms out from her sides, wet patches showing up on the legs of her light pants. It seems like Katherine is lost in her own world, forgetting for the moment that I'm even there. Almost as soon as the thought crosses my mind, though, she turns around, running backwards for a few steps. "C'mon, Charly!" So I speed up and catch her, landing with a soggy splat on a sandbar right beside her.

"Nice, eh?" I mean the weather, the sea, the smells, the sounds—everything. I like the shore, but I've never seen it so—I don't know. It's hard to describe. Fresh, maybe. Like we're the only ones here. No, better. Like we're the first ones here.

Katherine grins at me and ties her scarf tighter. "More than nice. It's glorious!" For an instant, the grin disappears, and her tone serious, she tells me, "Thank you, Charly."

The wind catches the floppy brim of my hat, threatening to carry it away. I bring my hand down on the crown, holding it to my head and smile at her. "Race you to the capes?"

Katherine doesn't answer, but her grin returns, and she starts at a full-out run. She's gotta be twice as old as me, but she's a lot taller, so chances are good she'll beat me there. But that's okay. She doesn't get out much.

I run faster, narrowly avoiding a rock and a broken shell, and hitting more water than I'd like to as those sandbars get further and further apart. I can hear my heart pumping in my ears and feel my skin tingle as the blood tries to reach my fingers and toes. I'm watching my feet, so I nearly run into Katherine when she stops dead in front of me. I stumble, coming to an awkward stop on a narrow strip of sand, bracing my hands on my knees to keep from toppling over. Katherine stares straight ahead, no more smile, her mouth slightly open.

"What?" I breathe the word out on a hard exhalation.

She doesn't answer for a long while, and when she does, her words are very quiet, almost drowned out by the swoosh of the waves kissing the sand then backing shyly away and returning over and over again on into forever. "It's just there's so many memories here. It's like they're crushing my heart." She lifts a hand to her chest, then looks at me and smiles weakly. It's like she's embarrassed.

"It's okay, y'know. To feel sad, I mean." I've never talked this way to an adult before, and now the words are sticking to the inside of my throat like dry popcorn. Still, I have to say it, have to make her feel better and try to let her know I understand. "If all of a sudden you landed me in my old backyard in Alberta under that one big poplar tree, I'd fall down in the grass or snow and just bawl!" It's true. Whenever I think about it, my eyes tear up, and my heart feels like it'll burst. I miss it so bad, but it's over. Gone. Kaput.

Katherine lays her hand on my shoulder, and neither of us says a thing. We just stand there looking out over the strait, and it crosses my mind that maybe I'm starting to love it as much as my old backyard—only different. When we turn back and head towards our abandoned shoes and the house, Katherine starts to talk.

"I'd bring Robert down here all the time for little walks in the sunshine. To get us both out of the house for a bit."

At the sun-bleached log, we sit down and pull our shoes back on. I start to get up, but my friend stays seated, so I decide I can wait to leave too.

"On a day just like this one, I walked with my baby in my arms." She laughs, sharp-edged and hard, short. "He was curious about the gulls. They'd fly low over the water, and little Robert would turn his whole head to follow them. He wouldn't just move his eyes—and he was so wobbly still, so young."

A tear appears in the corner of her eye, and as it trickles down her face, it sparkles in the sun. The ghost wipes at it with the back of her hand, but a wet splotch stays there on her face. I look down at my feet, at the shoes I've just laced up. I keep the heels together and move the toes apart to make what I think looks like a huge duck footprint in the red sand.

"I'm sorry," I mumble. "I'm sorry the shore makes you sad, and I'm sorry your baby died."

At this, Katherine reaches across the smooth white wood and grabs my hand. She smiles at me, and I can't believe she's not alive.

When we get nearer the house and have made our way up that steep sandy bank to the mowed lawn, something catches my eye that I didn't notice earlier in the backyard. There's a metal cross sticking out from those thick blue flowers growing close against the foundation of the O'Leary house.

Ten

Somehow my binder flipped open, and all my science notes and handouts spilled out into my locker, my name, Charly Pederson, scrawled along the tops of lots of those loose pages. It's been that kind of day. I scoop them up from where they're piled in the bottom of my locker and spread them out on the floor, where I can sort through them. The hallway's nearly empty, and the janitor is pushing her wide broom down the opposite side of the hall.

"Hey!" she calls to me, her voice thick and rough from years of smoking. "Use this. I gotta get this hall cleaned." She tosses me a smallish black garbage bag.

I stuff my papers into it, sling my backpack over my shoulder and, carrying the bag with my papers and binder in it, make my way towards the main doors.

"Char!" I turn at the sound of Derek's voice. He half-runs the length of the orange-tiled hall to catch up to me. "What's with the garbage bag? Nice accessory. Stylish."

"Shut up," I tell him, but with a smile. "My science binder broke. What're you still doing here?"

"Detention. Had to finish some work. No biggie." He

stops just before the doors, drops his backpack and zips up his coat. "You busy now?"

"Not really. Why?"

Derek pushes one of the doors open and holds it while I go through. He hesitates to tell me what he wants to do, so I press him by asking again, "Why?"

"Well, uh, the thing is," begins Mr. Articulate, "I'm kinda, uh, wondering..."

"Oh, just spit it out already!" After this day, my low math mark and Dennis's stupid comment about my glasses, my mood can't handle Derek's stammering.

"Do you think I can meet Katherine? I mean, at least try and see what happens?"

I shrug, act nonchalant, but I'm actually a little surprised at his request. I didn't think he was really interested in getting to know any ghosts. "Sure. We can try, if you want. But Grammie can't meet her. And Katherine's told me that I'm the only one she's been able to—" How do I put this? "—be herself with, if you know what I mean. So far, it's only me who can see her and talk with her."

"Wanna go now?" He sure does seem eager. Maybe he's psyched himself up or something.

"I can, but I want to stop by home and drop this stuff off. You can leave your backpack at my house if you want to."

With our stuff stowed at Grammie's and each with a baggie of her gingersnaps, we head out towards the shore. Derek is chatty as we walk along, and I have to move fast to keep up with him. He's walking backward in front of me so that he can see me while we talk.

I tell him, "Katherine told me she used to know Grammie. It was interesting." It's a little warmer today, and the wind's down. I'm not even wearing my mitts. They're forecasting snow, but it's hard to believe it's going to happen any time soon. "Grammie's told me about knowing Katherine, but it's different to hear it from someone else, y'know?"

My cousin falls into step beside me. "Yeah. Grammie's got some good stories. You should get her to write them down."

"Me? Why don't you get her to write them down?" I think I know his answer, but I want to hear him say it.

He shrugs. "You two talk differently from the way I do—you could talk to her about writing. She'd take your advice. She listens to you."

There it is. The answer I wanted.

"I can believe that the O'Leary place is haunted. Everybody's said that forever. But I have trouble believing you've been hanging out with a ghost." This is what Derek said when I told him about my visits with Katherine. I'm thinking he must be feeling a little more convinced of my own friendship with Katherine to be asking to meet her. I don't think it can happen, but you never know. I didn't think it could happen to me, and it did.

Katherine's house is in sight now, the sun lighting it up, making the building warm and friendly against its backdrop of blue sky. The walk is easy on this warm November day. Derek's unzipped his jacket, and my back's starting to feel a bit warm under my sweater and coat. The shore road is quiet. Only one car has driven by us, the driver waving as she passed then looking back at us in her rearview mirror.

"Can I ask you a question?" I say.

He kicks at a stone, and we both watch it bounce on down the asphalt to finally veer into the grass at the side of the road. "Go ahead. Shoot."

"How does Auntie Cindy get along with Grammie?"

"Mom?" Again, my cousin lifts his shoulders. "Not bad, I guess. Not like you and Grammie...or even like you and me." He looks over at me. "Why?"

"Oh, I dunno." I'm not sure what I want to know from him. "It's just that things are sort of...weird between Mom and Grammie. Like they get on each other's nerves." I think about it for a second longer and add, "Or maybe like they're competing, trying to show the other that they're smarter or know the right thing to do all the time."

"That *is* weird," Derek agrees. "But it sounds like what Mom and Grammie do, too."

"Does it ever make you wonder how we'll be with our moms when we're older? I mean, will we be friends with them, or will it be tense like it is around Grammie's now?"

Derek doesn't look at me. He stares down the road instead and into the distance. "Hard to say. I don't think about it much. I can't really picture my mom and me when I'm older."

"No, I s'pose I can't picture Mom and me in a few years, either. I just hope it's better than it is now."

We're nearing the yard around Katherine's place when Derek stops dead in his tracks. He points, his arm straight out, his index finger rigid and insistent. "Charly! Look! Do you see that? Up there in the window!"

Eleven

I shield my eyes from the sun with my left hand and look to where Derek points. I spot Katherine just in time to see her let go of the lace curtain she's pulled aside. I wave, but she doesn't wave back. Maybe she doesn't see me. Instead, her form retreats from the nursery window and she disappears, the lace curtain falling back into place.

"Is that her?" Derek's voice is about two octaves higher than usual. It sounds pretty funny.

"Yeah. That's her. Do you think she saw us?" I glance over at him and notice that he looks a little green around his mouth, and the rest of his face is really pale. "You okay?"

He shakes his head and chuckles. "I've never seen her before. Lots of people have. Mom claims she has—and more than once, too. Freaky."

In Katherine's front yard, there's a brisk breeze that wasn't with us on the road. Brisk *and* cold, with that salty edge to it. There's a thick layer of frost on the veranda steps, which are dangerous at the best of times, all rotten and falling in like they are. Now we've got to be really careful.

I ask Derek, "Do you still want to go in? We don't have to."

"No, I still wanna go in," he grins crookedly, "But I gotta admit I'm a little worried now that I might really meet her!"

I grin back and solidly pat his shoulder. "Won't happen. Don't worry."

As usual, the doorknob screeches something awful, and when we open the door, it wails like a cat whose tail's just been stepped on. "That's a pleasant sound," Derek murmurs sarcastically. I see him run the palms of his hands down the legs of his jeans. Then he rubs the back of his neck.

"You nervous?" I ask.

"Nah." He tells me. "Just cold." I don't believe him. I know nervous when I see it.

Inside the door, I'm surprised again by the old smells of mildew and decay. I've been here so many times when this house has been cleaner than Grammie's place—way cleaner—so it's easy to forget what it is really like. Old and falling slowly apart.

"It kinda smells in here." Derek stops a little ways into the entry, and I close the door noisily behind us.

I lead the way in the direction of the kitchen. Everything is dark and depressing, but my cousin doesn't comment on this as he does the smell. He's never seen the countertops new and polished clean, never experienced the warm, yeasty scent of pans of bread dough rising beside the stove or the tart, not-too-sugary tang of homemade lemonade on his tongue. It's not his fault, but Derek only knows this place in the now. He just sees one side of it. I realize that I'm lucky to know it the way I do, and even if it looks bad right this moment with its dust and dirt and dark, at least I know that somewhere else it still exists clean and new and lived in.

"It's colder in here than it is outside," Derek says, brushing past me into Katherine's parlour.

I agree. "It is. It's like the building holds on to the cold, keeps it in."

Derek stands beside the old organ, reaches out and pulls the cover back up over it again. "Looks pretty much the same as when we were in this place before." He shoves his hands deep in his pockets.

"I don't like it here when it's all shabby and old." I step into the middle of the room and take a good look around, remembering. "You should see how this room looks to me when I come here to visit Katherine. Way different."

Derek's moving around the periphery of the room, keeping his hands wedged in his coat pockets, not touching anything. My hands are in my pockets, too. I don't feel like hanging out here for too long. It's freezing cold, and it's also getting me down. I want to be somewhere warm. Without Katherine here, this place is just downright lonely.

At the tall window between the bookshelves and the wood box along the south wall, Derek pushes the heavy, dusty draperies aside, and some pale light leaks into the room. He must be calming down, because he turns to me and suggests, "Maybe we should head upstairs. You could at least show me the room she was standing in."

"Sure." I lead the way up the wide, dim staircase. I'm not thrilled about visiting my least favourite room in the O'Leary house—the nursery, but I won't admit this to

89

Derek. Besides, you never know. We just might get to see Katherine. Only I wasn't just reassuring my nervous cousin when I told him it wouldn't happen. I don't think it will.

As soon as we get to the landing, I can see that the door to the nursery is open. The blind in there must be open, too, because a pale light is spilling through the doorframe.

"That's weird." I say it under my breath. Still, Derek hears.

"What?" He cocks his head and seems to be listening hard for something. "What's weird?"

"Oh, nothing much," I tell him. "Whenever I've been up here before, all the doors have been shut tight, that's all."

"Oh." We're in the hall now, and Derek motions to the open nursery door with his chin. "Is that the room I saw her in?"

I nod and lay my hand on the glass doorknob, freezing cold to my touch. Swinging the door open, I invite Derek in. "After you." He hesitates for barely a moment then brushes past me.

"This is the baby's room," he says. Derek remains by the door, taking the room in with his eyes.

"Yep. Usually the blinds are all closed, too." I move towards the window, telling my cousin, "This is where she was when we saw her." As I move the lace curtain aside, Derek steps up beside me, standing a little too close. I'm about to tease him about being chicken and needing me to protect him, when the idea is frozen solid in my mind by the shock of what I see there on the window pane. Written in the fog with a fingertip are the words, *Hi Charly! I can see you!*

Twelve

T here they are. Right where the hill rises."

"By that tree?" I can't tell one headstone from another, and the sun is cutting across the sky and slanting straight into my eyes. I think I'm starting to see the point of wearing a floppy hat. Mine's in my closet at home.

"Yes." Grammie points. "Just to the right of it. There."

The grasses in the cemetery have been clipped short, and they crunch under our shoes as we walk. I see the place she means now. I'd been trying to spot three separate stones. Two big ones and a smaller one for baby. That's why I missed it. One long granite stone, dark grey and smooth, with the name cut deep and sure: O'Leary.

Grammie pulls her coat tighter around her body, and I wish I had worn my mitts and toque. There's no cement pad covering the gravesite, no flowers, no picket fence like you see around some of them. Just the stone. We sit down on the bench beneath the maple tree, its bare branches spreading wide against the harsh blue sky, and I think I can feel the thick layer of frost melt into my jeans. From here, we've got a good view of the little white church, Grammie's car parked in the gravel lot on the other side of the fence, a low black chain slung loosely between short metal posts less than a metre tall surrounding the whole cemetery. It's all out in the middle of the countryside.

"Do they use that church any more?" I glance over at Grammie. Her cheeks are getting red, and I suppose mine are, too. The wind is nippy.

"Now and then, for special occasions; Christmas Eve and Easter services, weddings, sometimes funerals. I used to think it would be romantic if your mom got married here." Grammie pauses here for a moment, her eyes focused on the old, straight building, then continues, "But she left, moved to Toronto and met your dad."

I nod. "She worked at the oil company, doing filing and answering phones. She hated it!" I know how the story goes. I'd heard it lots of times before they split up, back when they still got along and liked to talk about how they met. It's been a while since I heard that story.

Grammie laughs. "That she did, that she did. You probably know that your grampie and I were married here?"

"No. I didn't know that." I stand up and move towards the gravestone, feeling the cold even more against the damp denim of my pants.

"That was a long time ago now. Somehow it doesn't seem like it, though. Time goes fast, Charly. You'll see." She joins me in front of the stone. Again, we're facing into that wind.

"So, they're all buried here? Katherine and her husband and the baby?"

"Mmm-hmm," is Grammie's answer. The names and dates are there, etched deep and clear and dull compared to the shiny surface of the stone.

Thomas Johnston O'Leary: 1915-1971
Katherine Margaret O'Leary: 1927-1955
Robert Thomas O'Leary:
December 1953-March 1954

"He must've arranged for this to be set up before he died." She chuckles and explains, "That'd be just like old Thomas O'Leary. He'd want to make sure appearances were kept up, even after he was dead and gone. Nothing other than the stone here, though, and them beneath us." Grammie touches the toe of her sneaker to the ground at my feet. I step back quickly, not liking the idea of standing on dead people, especially when one of them's a friend of mine.

In response to my sudden backward movement, Grammie tells me, "It's all right, honey. You think they care where you stand?" To illustrate her point, she steps right up to the headstone. "They're gone. To them, it doesn't matter. They're free." Then she puts both her hands on the stone's rough and uneven top, still looking at me, half-smiling, kind of smug like Grammie gets when she knows something you don't. I can't stand that about her. It reminds me of Nikki.

All of a sudden, her face changes. That smug smile is

gone, and although her eyes still look my way, they're glassy and wide, and I can tell she can't see me. "Grammie?" Her body goes stiff, and she starts to shake all over, her eyes bulging and staring in my direction. Strangling, choking sounds come from her throat. Not loud noises, but loud enough for me to hear that she's having trouble breathing. "Grammie!" I grab hold of her arm and tug hard, loosening her grip on the granite. I keep pulling till she's back a couple metres, away from the gravesite.

"What was that?" I'm shouting. "Grammie? What's wrong?" I let go of her. She looks stunned, and it takes a second or two, but finally her eyes focus again, and she shakes her head and her hands, like she's trying to shake off whatever it is happened to her when she touched the stone. She doesn't say anything so, grabbing her arm again, I press her. "Grammie! Tell me!"

In true Grammie fashion, she dodges the question. Instead, she smiles at me weakly and says, "We better get back."

"But what happened to you? You look—scared or sick or something." She seems to be offended by this.

"I'm not scared, missy. I just don't know what happened, all right? So stop pushing me. I don't have an answer for you—or for me, for that matter." Her tone softens. "It's late. Let's go home and get supper on."

As we walk briskly back to her car parked there by the church, I count the number of times she looks back over her shoulder at the tombstone. Three.

Thirteen

The next day, early Monday morning, I'm sitting with my elbows on Katherine's square kitchen table with its four chairs, all painted white. There's a sugary cup of tea in front of me and a pot by my elbow in case I need a refill. Katherine's punching down bread dough at the low counter, talking over her shoulder to me as she works.

"Did you tell anyone about our adventure?"

"Yeah. Grammie."

Katherine stops her work for a moment and looks at me closely. "You really like this Grammie of yours, don't you?"

"I really do," I admit. "We get along—like you and I get along—even though she's an adult. An *old* adult. And she understands stuff, you know?"

"Stuff like what?" She has her hair piled on top of her head with what must be about a million bobby pins all hidden and now, as she pounds the dough, strands of it come loose and fall into her eyes. Her cheeks are flushed, and even though there's a foot of snow in her front yard, the kitchen is sweltering.

"You know. Dead people not being…" What're the right words? "Not quite dead."

"Like me?"

I shift in my chair and suddenly wish I hadn't gotten up so early to come over here before school. "Uhhh…I guess."

She sighs, rinses her hands in the sink and wipes them on her apron. She puts a damp tea towel over the pasty-white dough before coming over to the table with her own teacup and joining me. After what seems like a long time, she finally says, "I'm a little more than 'not quite dead.' I'm stuck in purgatory, that's where I am. Just plain stuck."

I try to change the subject. "We got some snow, too, but not as much as you." She ignores this and keeps right on talking.

"Except for that afternoon on the beach, I haven't been able to bring myself to leave here, either to die or to live."

"We can go back to the shore any time you want now that we know you're okay with it."

She stirs a teaspoon of sugar into her cup with a muted clinking sound and sets her spoon on the edge of her saucer. This place of hers is so fancy.

"Yes, that's true, and I'm happy about it, but I can't leave without you. Without my escort." She lifts her cup and, eyeing me levelly over the top of it, finishes her thought. "Like a prisoner."

"It's like you've grounded yourself."

She laughs a bit at this. "Have you ever been grounded?"

"Once, but only for three days. It was supposed to last a week, but I think Mom and Dad forgot about it." That was back before we moved here, when they were fighting a lot and going to see the counsellor who obviously didn't help much—or enough. I'd gone over to Allie's to watch movies, and when it got late, I stayed over and didn't call home. I didn't forget, either. Just didn't bother. Nikki and I got away with a lot during that last year because we could. Mom and Dad didn't seem to notice what we did, but I guess not coming home one night got their attention. "They were going through their own stuff. My sister, Nikki, she's been grounded a lot more than I have."

Katherine nods as if she understands. "She's older."

"Yup. And prettier. Very popular."

"Boyfriends?"

"Mmm-hmm. They're usually the reason she gets grounded."

"Just wait. In a couple of years, you'll be the one getting grounded all the time." I smile at her and take another drink of my tea. I don't say anything, because I doubt it. Our family's grounding days are long gone, and I can't tell if this makes me feel relieved or sort of sad. It's both, I guess.

Still holding her cup, Katherine leans back into her chair, and even though I don't look at her, I can feel her watching me again. Finally, she asks, "Who do you look more like? Your mother or your father?"

I don't have to think about it. "My dad, definitely. He's got dark hair and lighter skin and bad eyesight. He's pretty tall, so maybe someday…" I shrug and give her a half-smile. "How about you? More like mom or dad?"

"Mother. Especially now that I'm older. Here. I'll show you what I mean." She stands up and pushes in her chair. "Bring your tea—and the pot."

I follow Katherine through the parlour and into the formal dining area with its huge, heavy dining room suite, its sideboard and towering china cabinet. Even when she flicks the switch for the chandelier, it stays dark in here. I set my cup and the teapot down on a corner of the immense table and ask Katherine, "Mind if I pull up the blinds?"

I'm surprised when she tells me not to, then she gives me this explanation: "I don't like the snow, Charly. The gloom of winter is the last thing I want to deal with today—and I'll have to soon enough."

I sit down in a chair near where I set my cup, careful not to sit on the lace cloth hanging over the table's edge. From the cupboard space beneath the sideboard, Katherine brings out a thick black album. She sits down beside me and opens it up. There's no plastic holding the black and white photographs in place on the sturdy paper pages. Instead, each picture's four corners is anchored onto the page with a black triangle. In that book is most of Katherine's life. On the first page, there's a picture of a girl who, at first, I think must be Katherine, standing outside a house and holding a baby girl dressed in a long, white gown. "Who's that baby you're holding?"

"That's not me. *I'm* the baby. That's my mother. Sophia Sowden. That's the day of my baptism."

"Wow. You do look like your mom. Almost exactly."

I move my face closer to the photo and see that Sophia's hair is a shade or two darker than Katherine's. It's a detail that's easy to miss in black and white.

"It's strange," Katherine says softly. "From the side, when I'm looking at your profile, you remind me of me sometimes."

I just laugh and shrug, but to me it's a big compliment, because Katherine's very pretty. Better looking than I'm sure I'll ever be, but her comment makes me happy anyway, even if I don't believe it. I point to the baby Katherine in the picture. "Is that why you're dressed like that? Because you're being baptized?"

"That's right. And that's me at three with my brother Ronald in the wagon by the oak tree in our backyard in Halifax, and here we are at our Grandfather Sowden's farm. This was taken just before my sisters were born. Twins. Elizabeth and Victoria, but we usually called them Lizzy and Vikki. After that, mom had two more boys, Francis and Dwayne. She died when Dwayne was born."

"Why?"

Katherine doesn't look at me, instead keeps her eyes focussed on the page in front of her. "The doctor at the time thought that maybe she was ill and that her body couldn't handle another birth. Or maybe she was too old to be having any more children."

"How old was she?"

Katherine thinks for a moment. "Thirty-six."

"My mom was thirty when I was born. Thirty-six is young to die."

Katherine turns the pages, and I keep asking questions.

She shows me where she went to school in Halifax, where she used to skate every winter with her younger sisters, more pictures of her father's father's farm and, later, a picture of his fresh grave sprayed with flowers, people standing around in the snow, dark shapes against a grey background. I see a picture of her before the spring dance at her high school, holding the arm of a tall young man with fair hair on the steps of her father's house. "Is that your husband?"

When she answers, Katherine sounds almost shocked. "No!" But then she laughs and tells me, "I can tell you've never seen a picture of Thomas." She skips a couple of pages and brings us to their wedding day. "There. See the difference? No mistaking them, is there?"

The misunderstanding does seem funny now, seeing Thomas O'Leary there in the upper left-hand corner, his dark, unsmiling eyes staring right through me out of that really good-looking face. His hair is dark, probably black, like his moustache, eyebrows and long eyelashes. Nikki would call this guy hot, and I guess I would, too, if he wasn't Katherine's dead husband.

"Handsome, isn't he?"

"I guess…"

"Gerald, the other one, was much kinder." She turns back to his picture and gently touches his image with her fingertip. He has a soft face, a little round, young.

"So, what happened? He wasn't your type?"

Finally, she closes the thick album. "He wasn't Father's type. He wanted for me—and for him— someone with solid business interests. Gerald worked in his father's pharmacy. After high school, he went to Boston to study, and I heard that he came back to Halifax to take over his father's store. A lowly job, in my father's eyes, though I'm sure Gerald's been quite comfortable, maybe even happy."

"Couldn't you have run off with Gerald? You know? Gone with him when he went to Boston?"

"Yes, in hindsight that was an option, a choice I could've made, but back then it seemed unthinkable to just up and leave." Then her eyes get this faraway look, and her mind seems to wander. Katherine mumbles, "But when I first realized that I, that we were…" She stops abruptly and looks at me as if she just remembered I was there. My ghost friend shakes her head, and I notice her eyes glistening as she continues telling her story, a story I now get the feeling she's editing for my benefit. "I suppose I didn't want to disobey my father but, more than that, I also realize now that I was afraid, afraid of what I didn't know, afraid of moving to the United States, just plain afraid of everything." She lifts her hands, a frustrated gesture, and brings them back down on either side of the album. "Father and my siblings and I had a nice home together, and we all got on fairly well. So I stayed. In the end, it was my decision." Then she looks at me hard, clasps her hands on the table in front of her and leans in towards me. "When it comes right down to it, Charly, it's been my decisions that have landed me here. Truth is, everyone's responsible for their own choices." She leans back in her tall-backed chair and sighs. "I've got no one to blame but myself."

Fourteen

No one to blame for what?"

Katherine doesn't answer me but instead stands up, closes the album and puts it back beneath the large, dark-wood sideboard. She gently shuts the cabinet and begins walking out of the dining room. She crooks her finger in my direction as she walks, already in the parlour, cutting through to the kitchen. "Come upstairs with me. You need to know the whole story."

I push in my chair, its legs moving unwillingly on the rug covering the polished wood floor. I think I know exactly where she's taking me, and when Katherine's hand touches the closed nursery door, I know I'm right. Then she says something that surprises me.

"You were in here with your grandmother, and I wanted so badly to tell you the story then, to just come out, get real, step into your grandmother's time like you can move into mine, but I couldn't. She seems really kind. Is she funny?"

"You mean is she weird?"

Katherine laughs at this. "No! I mean, does she have a good sense of humour—like you?"

"I suppose. Sometimes."

"Hmm. I wish I could get to know her like I've gotten to know you." We're standing on that braided rug in the centre of the room, gloomy but not as dark by far as the dining room had been. She smiles at me. Then, unexpectedly, Katherine touches my cheek with her cold hand and takes it away just as quickly.

She flicks on the light switch by the doorframe and, as she did in the dining room, leaves the blinds drawn blocking out the drear of the day. Everything looks the same as it did a week or so ago. The rocking chair is still beneath one of the windows, but neither of us sits down. Katherine lays her hand on the short dresser, leaves it flat for a moment then touches the fur on the teddy bear's ear.

Nervously, I tell her, "I like that bear."

"I do too. I bought it for someone else, a baby girl a long time ago. I never had the chance to give it to her."

"So you gave it to Robert?" That's me, always stating the obvious.

"That's right. And this is my little boy's room. Your grandmother's right. He died." She seems to be examining the fire engine while she talks to me. As curious as I've been, now I'm not sure I want to hear the story. But Katherine can't read my mind, so she begins.

"Thomas was away—he was away a lot—and Robert was one day short of four months old. He'd been fine up till then. Fat and healthy, a big baby. He was starting to get a little fussy, crying and fidgeting more often, but nothing very extreme. Just baby stuff. You know."

But I don't know, don't know much about babies at all.

Nikki's taken a babysitting course, and back home, she used to babysit lots up and down our block. I went babysitting one time with Allie, but she did everything with the little girl, who wasn't a baby. She might've been two or three years old. I mostly watched TV while they played.

Katherine takes her hand off the dresser, leaving the fire engine and teddy bear alone, and turns in my direction. "He wouldn't settle down to nap that afternoon, then could barely keep his eyes open while I fed him an early supper." The light above us is reflected in the wet of Katherine's eyes. I shift my weight from my left foot to my right and suddenly, I don't know what to do with my hands hanging at my sides. I clasp them uncomfortably behind me. "I put him down to sleep early, hating to because I thought he'd be awake at four o'clock in the morning." Now a tear slips out and makes it about halfway down her cheek before she swipes at it. I pretend not to see and focus my eyes on the tall crib in the corner.

Katherine swallows hard, but even so, it sounds like she's choking on her words. "I checked on Robert before I went to bed around ten." She gasps and forces the next sentence out in one long, whining breath. "He was already dead."

I look at my feet. I wish I was home. I don't know what to say. "Oh, that's sad."

It sounds stupid, but Katherine doesn't seem to mind. She straightens herself and tells me, "Let's go to my room. I'll dig out something for you to wear." Over her shoulder, she gives me what mom calls a knowing look, only I don't know anything. "We're going to need to head outside."

From her tall bureau by the window, Katherine pulls out the bulkiest wool sweater I've ever seen. Then, from up on the shelf in her closet, she brings down a red wool toque and matching mitts that don't quite clash with the blues and oranges in the sweater, but that don't match at all, either. Katherine must recognize something in the way I look at the articles of clothing she hands me because, as she does, she admits, "I know, I know. They're ugly as sin, but they're warm, and you'll be thankful for that when we reach the backyard."

She helps me pull the sweater on over my head. Katherine laughs when my head comes through, my hair sticking up with enough static electricity to sustain a small village. "Lost your glasses?"

"Yep. That always happens." I reach up under the sweater, already beginning to feel like I'm going to roast alive. My glasses are stuck in a deep fold about halfway down the front of the inside.

"How come you don't take them off first?"

I shrug. "I forget, I guess." Now she sounds like Nikki, trying to tell me the right way to do things, so I say, "Don't you ever forget anything?"

But she's not my sister, and she shakes her head slightly. "Charly, for the life of me, I can't remember anything I need to and can't forget anything I want to. Like the night Robert died."

"You can't forget or you can't remember?" We're heading back downstairs, and I'm one step behind all the way. She's taking the stairs quick, and I'm glad. I can feel the sweat under my arms and on the back of my neck.

"Both." We're in the foyer now, and Katherine brings her long fur coat down from the rack in the corner next to the door. "Of course, I wish I could forget he died, that he was ever born. The memory hurts too much, hasn't stopped hurting for all this time. And I wish I could forget what I did that night."

"Why? What did you do?" I have to half run as I follow her down the short hall into the kitchen. Katherine doesn't answer my question, instead tells me, "We'll go out this way. It'll be easier." The heavier inside door groans as she yanks it open and unhooks the screened door that leads out to her vegetable patch in the summer—whenever it decides to happen around here. There's not much snow on the veranda right outside the kitchen door, but the stairs leading down to the yard are a different story. They're covered in snow, so that I can't see the three individual steps, just a short snow ramp where they used to be. I look over the yard and across the road to that old barn. The snow is perfect. Not a track in it, and the old horse is gone from the pasture. Maybe inside somewhere warm, maybe dead, maybe not born yet. Who knows? I've figured out that I can't know anything about how time works here. Or life, or death, for that matter.

Katherine's wearing boots, dress boots that don't look very warm and zip up on the side, so she steps down into the snow first. For a dead person, she sure is careful. I'm wearing my runners, so I'm happy for tracks to follow, and I step down into the first two prints she makes. Her feet aren't much bigger than mine. She leads me along the east side of the house, and in some places, the snow is up to my thighs, the last foot of Katherine's fancy coat resting on top of the snow as she trudges forward.

"Are we going to the well?"

This time she answers, pausing to say, "No. Not that far. You cold?"

"I'm okay." And I am until we round the corner of the house, and the wind off the strait hits us head on, slicing right through the too-bright sweater, determined to cut me in half. It forces my words and my breath back down my throat. I can't stay out here for long. As it turns out, I don't have to.

Katherine stops, and because I'm keeping my head down, I nearly walk into her back. "Here." She points at the snow drifted up along the foundation.

"I don't see anything."

Katherine bends down and with her mittened hands digs around, quickly exposing that rusty cross whose top used to poke out above the tall flax. "Yeah, I remember that! I thought it was to hold up flowers or something!" I'm yelling so she can hear me over the wind.

She yells back, "It's Robert! I buried him here! Blue flax for my baby boy!"

Fifteen

I pause at the door and take a deep breath, trying to get my story straight in my mind. I don't even know what time it is. All I know is that when I left Katherine's front yard, night fell like a hammer, and although the metre of snow had disappeared, that icy cold wind hadn't gone anywhere. On my way home, I actually wanted that disgusting sweater and the mitts and toque back. My fingers are freezing, and I can't feel my toes. I stomp my feet to try to get the circulation going, and as I do the porch light above my head flashes on, and the door flies open.

"Charly! Thank God!" Mom grabs me with both arms, pulling me in and hugging me hard all at the same time—like she used to when I was little. Her love feels good, and for a moment I forget the heap of trouble I'm going to be in. I hug her back and feel like crying, but I don't.

"Close the door, you two. It's not summer any more."

Mom holds me at arm's length, and I see a streak down her cheek reflecting the light of Grammie's entry. She pulls the door closed and locks the deadbolt, something I've never seen Grammie do. "Where've you been?"

The story I made up on the way home sucks. It goes

something like this: I didn't get all my work done so my teacher kept me in after school, only there was a staff meeting and she forgot I was in the room. I fell asleep, and everyone else went home. When I woke up, I came straight home. Lame. I get as far as saying, "My teacher kept me..." when Grammie, to my huge relief, interrupts.

"Forget it, Charly. Your mom knows everything. I told her when you didn't show up at school this morning."

Mom still hasn't let go of me, is holding each of my arms again, gripping me like she doesn't want me to get away ever again. It's not so bad. Her eyes look tired, black underneath, red around the rims. "Are you okay? I've been worried half to death." She runs her hands up and down the length of my arms, then lets her own arms fall to her sides.

"Yeah, I'm okay." I bend down and pry off my shoes without unlacing them. My toes tingle painfully, and wriggling them only makes it worse. My fingertips are aching, but not in the same tingling way. It's more of a dull, numb kind of hurt. "Sorry you were worried. I'm not usually gone long. Mostly, time seems to stop when I'm there, at the O'Leary place. Right, Grammie?" I turn my head towards her for confirmation.

She nods. "That seems to be the case, all right. So what happened this time?"

We go into the kitchen and sit down at Grammie's big oval table in its high-backed chairs. The clock on the wall over the table says six thirty. I can hear Nikki upstairs in her room, the music playing, her voice on the phone above it, lots of giggling and words I can't make out.

Grammie and Mom both look at me expectantly, and finally Grammie prompts, "Well?"

"How much does Mom know? Where should I start?"

Mom answers. "I know you visit Katherine, and that she's supposedly a ghost, the ghost of a young woman your Grammie used to know fifty-plus years ago. I know time changes when you go to the O'Leary place alone. And that everything stays the same, including time, when you are accompanied by someone else." Then she shrugs. "I'm not sure I believe it."

"Okay." I don't know what else to say. I'm tired and half-frozen. I take a sip of the tea Grammie poured for me and notice for the first time that I'm starving. Remembering the most interesting detail of my adventure, I turn to Grammie and blurt out. "I found out today where Baby Robert's really buried." I take another hot gulp of tea and feel it warm my insides.

"You mean he's not in the cemetery? What does the stone say? Where is he then?" Grammie wants to know. Mom's elbows are on the table, and she's leaning in to hear me. She hasn't touched her tea. Tonight, I'm suddenly visible.

"He's in the flowerbed along the back of the house." I pause for effect, watching both their faces before I add, "Under the flax."

Grammie sits back and looks disgusted, unaffected by my melodrama, but I plod forward. I want them both to hear about my friend's sadness. To actually know about it.

"It's really hard for Katherine. She went upstairs to his nursery one night, missing him, and Robert was there in his crib, wriggling his legs in the air and smiling up at her. She had him back for a day. And even though she sat in that rocker by his crib all night long, in the morning he was back in the flowerbed."

Grammie and Mom both take in a short, sharp breath, and Mom's hands shoot up to cover her mouth. She removes them to whisper, "That's terrible," to which Grammie replies curtly, "What do you care? You don't believe a word of it. Remember?"

Mom shoots Grammie a look. "It's just...I...it's a sad story, real or not."

"Humph." Grammie grunts and shifts her weight around the seat of her chair. "Like watching a soap opera, I suppose." She looks towards the door into the sun porch and leaves her attention there, as if she's expecting someone to arrive any minute. She's not, though.

My tea is getting cold, but I don't drink any more of it, just keep my hands wrapped around the mug to thaw out my fingers. We're all quiet for a bit, each of us looking at our hands as if we've noticed them for the first time. Grammie is the first to break this silence.

"Okay. So the baby's in the flowerbed—whether your mom believes it or not." An accusing look in Mom's direction. Mom doesn't look back, but I can tell she knows that Grammie's watching her. Instead, she takes a long drink of tea and refills her cup from the old brown teapot with the chipped spout, then slumps back tiredly in her chair, her hands folded over her belly.

At this point, I'm too exhausted to care whether or not Mom believes the stories I have to tell. Maybe she thinks

I'm like Nikki, that I've been out skipping school all day with some boy. Doesn't matter anyway. You can't usually change what people choose to think about you. I don't look at Mom when I talk. Just at Grammie. The stories are for her. "Katherine's afraid to leave the O'Leary place without me."

Grammie asks, "Why?"

I shrug, push my tea away and look around the kitchen. "I don't know. Guess she's scared of what she doesn't understand. Afraid of her future as a dead person. Afraid to be alone."

Both Grammie and I look when Mom says, "Just like the rest of us, I suppose." She turns her head away, stares off towards the living room and tries to hide the fact that her eyes are brimming with tears about to topple. One blink, and we'll all have to swim. The light from the three light fixtures secured above the ceiling fan over the table reflects off her full eyes.

Her tears tell me that maybe Mom is getting it after all. "Yeah, I think so. Kathcrine's just like a real person. Lonely and mixed up."

As I stand up from my chair, I realize I don't hear the rumbling disjointed noise of Nikki's stereo. She appears at the bottom of the stairs just as I'm making my way over to the refrigerator. She doesn't wait for an answer, says instead, "Mark asked if I could come over for a bit to help him with his English essay."

With my head in the fridge, I mumble, "He needs all the help he can get."

Nikki tosses a "Shut up!" in my direction then asks

Mom, "Can I go?" I realize that she probably doesn't know I was missing, that Mom and Grammie never told her and that she didn't ask. Nice family we've got going here.

"Till what time?"

"About ten."

"Make it nine thirty."

"Okay," she answers in a pouty voice, and she vanishes in a cloud of perfume.

I've found some potatoes, green beans and a couple of hamburger patties on a plate in the fridge, and I pop it into Grammie's toaster oven. She hasn't yet updated her kitchen appliances to include a microwave. Wouldn't want to risk plunging too fast into the modern age.

I bring my plate back over to the table. Neither Mom nor Grammie have made any move to get up. With her eyes dry now, and her voice like stone, Mom accuses us, "Is it really worth all this?"

"Is what really worth all what?" Grammie answers her daughter's question with a question of her own, her own tone hard and cold. It's like they're competing to be the meanest. In some ways, they can be way worse than Nikki and me.

Mom lets out a kind of snort that instantly tells me she thinks Grammie's playing dumb. The hamburger patties are good. I cut them up and dip the little pieces in ketchup. Let them fight. I'm so hungry, I could gnaw off my arm.

"Is it really worth creating all these crazy stories about sad ghosts just to cover up?"

Grammie sounds genuinely surprised. "Cover up what?"

Mom throws her hands up in the air. She's frustrated. "I don't know! You tell me? What is it? What don't you want me to know? What are you trying to keep from me?" She plants her palms firmly and flatly on the tabletop and pushes herself up. "I know I haven't been the best one lately, but I'm still her mother." Then her face crumples like an old newspaper, and Mom sits back down all loose and rag doll-like. She lays her head on her arms and sobs.

I see other kids cry all the time, and it doesn't bother me that much. Not this way, anyway. And Nikki's always crying over one guy or another, but this is different. My face heats up, and I don't want to be there in the kitchen. My throat closes up, and my mouth gets all dry. I feel like I'm witnessing something I shouldn't, feel sort of ashamed to be there. I want to sink into the wall or into the floor. So much for enjoying my food.

It surprises me when Grammie reaches over and puts her hand on Mom's head. She starts slowly stroking her hair as if Mom was a kid again, and she makes soft shhhing sounds like you do for babies when they're crying. Then Grammie looks over at me, and unhappily I realize that I haven't disappeared.

"Hurry up and eat, girl. We're taking your mom here for a drive before your sister gets home."

"We can go now. I'm done." I take my plate over to the sink and go to find my coat.

Sixteen

M om pulls our SUV onto the patch of sparse gravel at the side of the road closest to Katherine's front gate. She turns off the ignition and comments, "I still don't understand why you dragged me out here. It looks spooky tonight."

She's right. Lots of times I've *felt* that the place was spooky, but it never looked so ghostly. In the full moonlight, the house's angles seem dipped in silver, while any flat surface looks black as deep, deep water. The thin layer of snow over everything gives the impression that the structure is hovering just above the ground.

Grammie explains, "We're going to show you around, put you in the place, tell you some more of the stories." She clamps a hand on Mom's shoulder from where she sits in the passenger seat. "Then if you want to believe, it's up to you. Whatever happens, I don't want you thinking that your daughter and I are not being honest with you. I can accept that you don't believe in ghosts. Lots of people don't, and that's fine, but I can't stand to think that you don't believe in us."

Mom doesn't say anything, just gets out of the

vehicle while Grammie flashes me a look over her shoulder and mouths to me, "Here goes."

The moon over the strait is full and the black shadow of the house engulfs the front yard. We walk around to the back, and as we do, the moonlight illuminates Mom and Grammie, so that I can see the strain on their faces. I wish I could be here alone to visit again with my friend, away from them, away from everything.

Of course, there's no flax. Just a thick brown tangle of dead grass and leaves, frosty and frozen stiff. Sticking out of all of this, along the back of the house, is the metal cross. With my mitts, I pull the mass of dead growth away from it so that we can have a better view of it. "Here it is."

"Sure enough," Grammie whispers and lays her hand on the cross, made sparkling white by the cold and the moonlight. And when she touches it, her face floods with sadness, and instantly she pulls her gloved hand away.

"What is it, Mom?" my mom asks Grammie, stepping up beside her quickly. "You not feeling well?"

When she answers, her voice isn't really solid, kind of broken up. "Yes...yes. I...I'm fine." But then she turns to me and confesses, "He's buried there, all right. I think that's what bothered me about our visit to the graveyard. Something seemed wrong. Dark. Like a harmful lie. He's not in the cemetery at all, is he?"

Slowly, I shake my head. "Nope. Katherine went a little crazy, and now she's so sad for it."

"Oh, come off it," Mom interjects, arms folded tight and close across her front. "You two are so cryptic." With that, she rolls her big brown eyes and tips her chin upward, the silver moon illuminating the right side of her face, and gasps. She thrusts her hand up in the air, pointing to one of the windows overlooking the strait. Thomas's office. "Who's that?" She almost yells it.

Grammie and I are focussing on that window before Mom's words are out, our eyes fixed on Katherine's shadowy figure holding the curtain out of the way and looking out into the night. Automatically, I wave and call out to her like I would to any friend I see across the street. But she ignores me, ignores the three of us actually, and continues to stare out over the glistening, shifting waters of Northumberland Strait. Soon after, she lets the curtain fall back over the window, and she turns away.

I put my hand on Mom's shoulder. "That's Katherine."

"So it is," she agrees. "So it is."

Grammie looks at me. "You want to go in and see her, tell her we've convinced your mom she exists?"

I nod. "I know I just saw her, but seeing her there in the window without her seeing me is driving me nuts."

"Okay. Go ahead. Your mom and I need to run home. In all the excitement, I think I left the kettle plugged in. We'll be back in ten. You be careful, okay?"

"You listen to your grandmother. Be careful—and be quick."

I can tell they're both nervous after my last long and very recent episode of being gone who-knows-where to see Katherine, so I'm grateful that they're letting me go. I'm wearing the heavy down jacket that used to belong to my Grampie. I feel and, no doubt look, like a gigantic turtle. "I will."

Mom and Grammie walk me around to the front of the house, and I walk them to the car just outside the fence, planning to re-enter on my own. They get into the car, and Mom starts to drive away slowly, watching me in her side mirror as Grammie stares over her shoulder, watching me. I think these two are making me nervous, or maybe it's just the eerie way Katherine's house looks tonight. Dark, abandoned, dead. I don't bother going through the gate but instead chance tripping on stray wires hidden under the snow and cut over the fallen-down fence. Luckily, I don't trip and, as it turns out, I don't need my great big turtle getup.

"Hi!" Katherine looks over her shoulder at the sound of my voice, her wide-brimmed straw hat tilting to one side as she does. She's kneeling on the green grass and working the soil around the tall flowers in her front beds.

"Charly!" She smiles at me and drops her trowel. Standing up, she brushes off her navy blue pants before asking, "What's with the coat? You expecting a storm?" Then she laughs at me, watching as I shrug off the heavy thing, letting it fall onto the lawn.

"It was snowing when I was here this afternoon! What did you expect me to wear?"

Her smile disappears, and she looks a little confused.

"What?" I want to know what she's thinking, why the blank look all of a sudden.

"Oh, it seems like a long time since I've seen you, that's all." Then she adds, "And it's always good to see you." She puts her arm around my shoulders and gives me a quick squeeze. It bugged me when she laughed at my coat, but now I feel better. Katherine makes it hard for you to stay mad at her.

"Can you stay awhile?" She asks me, and I recognize that desperate look in her eyes that belies the light tone of her voice.

"Not too long. My Mom and Grammie are waiting in the car."

"You should've brought them in! The four of us would've had such a good visit."

"They'd like to visit." I know Grammie would, but I'm pretty sure Mom would freak out. "But they can't get here the same way I can."

Katherine nods and seems to remember. "Let's go sit around back in the shade. It's such a gorgeous day!"

And it is. Hot even, and I wonder where all the snow went but, as I'm learning, there aren't a lot of answers here, and the seasons are free to arrive in any order they want. We walk around the west side of the house, where white sheets are hanging on the line. As we walk by, I let my hand glide flat over the fabric barely moving in the breeze and feel the damp cool. "Mom used to hang the sheets out during the summer back in Alberta. Makes them smell so good."

We sit down in the same white lawn chairs that make me slouch. I wonder if I'll ever be tall enough not to slouch in these deep chairs. Tonight—or today, I guess it is now—slouching feels good, natural in the heat. Katherine's moved the chairs to the west side of the yard, closer to the well. I glance over my left shoulder, and I can see the tip of the cross sticking out of the mass of flowering flax that surrounds it. The sight of it urges me to tell Katherine what just happened. I've never been good at broaching subjects gracefully, and so I blurt it out.

"Mom saw you!"

Her eyes are wide. "What? When?"

"Just now! She saw you just now in one of Thomas's office windows."

At first, I can't read her look. "Really? Just now?"

"Yes. Just now." I adjust myself in the deep chair. I'm starting to sweat. My body isn't used to summer time any more.

Katherine sits back and smiles, her face shaded by her broad brim, and the sparkling light of the strait is reflected in her eyes. "Isn't that something?" Then she sits up straight, looking alarmed.

"What's the matter?"

"I don't know. Listen. Can you hear that?"

Seventeen

W hat?" At first, I can't hear anything. Then, drifting on the air, the sound of very familiar voices. We both freeze and sit there straining to hear in the heat of the afternoon in Katherine's backyard.

"C'mon, Nik. There's no one around." It's Mark. He's whining, kind of pleading, but Nikki doesn't sound convinced. Helping him with his homework. Yeah, right.

"Not now, Mark. Can't we just walk for awhile? Talk a bit?"

"It's cold, and I don't wanna walk. C'mon!" They come around the east side of the house, the side where Katherine has her garden. Mark is pulling Nikki towards him, and she's pulling away. They look like half the couples in my junior high dance class, clutching each other, awkward and stumbling. Neither of them look our way, their eyes riveted on one another.

I know Nikki, and she looks mad. But then, so does Mark.

"Let go! Mark! Don't!" My sister plants both hands on his chest and shoves hard. Her boyfriend loses his balance and starts to fall backwards but shoots back up as if he's spring-loaded. I can't believe my eyes when he reaches out and around Nikki's neck, grabbing the hair at her nape. He forces her to the ground, and without my brain's permission, my legs start moving. I think I hear Katherine call, "Charly!" as I run towards them, but I'm not listening. All I hear for sure is Nikki's yelp of pain, and all I see is Mark standing over her.

Next thing I know, I'm up on his back with both my fists full of his hair. I'm thinking that it's surprisingly soft, even as he yells his pain and alarm. "What the—?" Nikki scrambles out of the way. She's looking at Mark struggling, and it's then I realize that she can't see me. I'm invisible! How great is that? As Mark falls to his knees under my weight, with new confidence I drive my knee into his spine until he's flat on the green grass. My sister just stands there, her arms hanging at her sides with her mouth flopped open. I scream, "Run, Nikki! Run!"

She hears this. I can tell, because her eyes open wide and she jumps straight up, turns around and dashes back past the full plants in Katherine's vegetable garden, her pink ski jacket a flash in the afternoon light. I push Mark's face down into the grass and keep my knee in the middle of his back.

I swear he's trembling. I don't say anything, just concentrate on holding him down until Nikki can get a good head start. When I guess it's safe, I let him up, leaping off his body and standing back as he whirls around, wild-eyed and crazy-looking in his unzipped winter coat, the summer sun lighting the yard around him.

It really is true! Mark can't see me. His eyes move

122

over the exact spot where I'm standing, but they don't stop there. He has no idea it's me so, just for kicks, I lean up near his face and yell, "Boo!" I've never seen anyone run faster in my life. What a day!

"Charly!" It's my turn to jump. Katherine is suddenly standing right beside me. "You sure showed him! Did you see the look on his face?" She laughs and pats my shoulder before asking, "Who are they? I think I've seen them before."

"That's my sister, Nikki, and her boyfriend, Mark."

"I hope he's not her boyfriend any more."

"Yeah. Me too." I breathe in the salt air. I feel good. Really good. "You might recognize them because I was with them that day we broke into your house. Sounds like you saw everything."

Katherine nods as we return to the lawn chairs. "It's true. Whenever anyone comes around, I can see them and hear them. Lots of times, I want to talk to them." She sighs. "It's hard. I just can't reach them—until you, that is." Then she tilts her head to one side. "There was someone else, a man, fairly soon after I died, I think. I'd seen him around town when I first moved here with my husband. He'd be staggering down the walk, everyone moving to the other side of the street as he approached. Once, I remember seeing him vomiting in an alleyway downtown." Katherine shakes her head like she's bringing herself back. "Anyway, after I died, and Thomas would be away on business, Alvin—that was the old guy's name—would break in and sleep in our bed. He was clever about it, too. Never left a trace of his presence. Was careful to clean up after himself and to close the door when he left." She chuckles and leans back into her chair. "But I knew he was there. I watched him, sometimes all night long. Just sat on the trunk at the foot of the bed while he slept, stinking up the room with his boozy snoring."

"So what happened with him?"

"One night, I followed him over to the sink when he went to get himself a glass of water. He whirled around and, when I saw his expression, I realized for the first time that he could see me! I'd assumed all along that I was invisible and, as it turns out, I mostly am, but not to him, not that night."

I sit forward in my chair. This is getting good. "What'd he do?"

She laughs again, loud and free this time. As she tells the story, her face captures some of Alvin's expressions. "First he yelled, then he dropped the glass. It shattered on the floor, and he yelled again. I tried to talk to him, get him to calm down. I certainly didn't want to scare him. I thought he might have a heart attack and die right there on my kitchen floor. I dreaded the possibility of spending eternity stuck in that house with the town drunk. He just shook his head at me and kept repeating, 'No such thing as ghosts. Got nothin' to be scared of. Ain't no such thing as ghosts.'"

In imitating Alvin, Katherine lowers her voice an octave or two. "I tried to explain that I didn't think I was a ghost, but he kept interrupting me, tuning me out. Finally, he made it to the front door and bolted across the lawn, tripping over his own feet twice.

"I locked the door and found I was able to clean up the glass. Thomas never suspected a thing."

"And then there was me."

"Yes. And then there was you." Katherine looks at me. "I suppose it goes without saying, but you're much better company."

"Gee, thanks."

Again, her laugh. "You're welcome."

She's happy, so I figure that now's as good a time as any. "Katherine? Do you remember talking to me about your baby? About Robert? And how he's not buried in the cemetery?"

"Yes, of course I remember." She sounds a bit too offended at my suggestion that she may've forgotten, and for a moment I wonder if she has. I keep going anyway and hope she really does remember.

"Grammie, Mom and I were talking about it. Maybe you *can* leave here, and you don't because you're so sad about Robert. Maybe you're just really, really scared." Katherine is still listening, so I just keep talking. "Mom didn't believe anything we were saying—until she saw you up in the window tonight. The look on her face! It *was* something! It's going to be hard for her to call Grammie crazy any more."

Katherine seems to be considering a point I've made for a moment, then she asks, "Well, is she?"

"Huh? Is she what?"

"You know. Is she…?" Katherine gestures, rotating her index finger in the direction of her right ear.

"Grammie? Crazy? No. Not really. I mean, not so much as you'd notice."

"You said I knew her. What's her name, this crazy grandmother of yours?" she asks through a crooked smile.

"Cosie McNickle."

Katherine's face lights up. "Oh! You *are* Cosie's grand-daughter! I thought maybe you were, and now I'm sure I can see the resemblance!"

"You mean I look like her?"

She tilts her head slightly and tells me, "Maybe a bit. But mostly it's the way you talk…and how you act."

I'm a bit relieved. I love Grammie but really don't want to look like her. "How do I act?"

"Brave, I suppose. Like you'll try anything just for the adventure."

What? I can't believe I'm hearing this. Does she know me at all? I'm the biggest chickencrap known to humankind! "Who? Me?" is all I manage to spit out. She just chuckles a bit, then stops when her eyes meet mine. Then she gets all serious both in her eyes and in her tone of voice.

"Yes. Of course, you." Katherine arches her eyebrows at me, the way she seems to a lot. "You seem surprised?" This is a question. Not a statement.

I shrug. "I dunno. I guess." She just sits there, waiting for me to say more. I sigh, forcing the breath out noisily through my open mouth. "It's not how I picture myself, okay?"

Katherine's glance moves out over the strait and, for a moment, she looks like she's thinking hard. "Hmm." Here it comes. "That's strange. I've always seen you as brave."

She smiles. "I suppose we're all entitled to our own perceptions."

I feel my face get hot. "Yeah, well, anyway…"

I'm happy when Katherine moves off the topic of me and onto the topic of her. "I never thought that it could be my fear that's keeping me here. I realize I'm very afraid, but I suppose I assumed that every dead person is afraid. It seems natural to want to leave but also to feel too scared." She shrugs and adds to her thoughts. "It could be that I'm punishing myself, you know. After all, it's my fault that my son's tucked away in an apple box under the dirt of the flowerbed."

It seems like a good a time as any to bring the next issue up. "Grammie and I took a trip out to the cemetery. You know. The one by the little United Church. The headstone there says that all three of you are buried there. You, the baby, and your husband."

Her eyes widen slightly as she focuses in on my face. "Does it? Well, I'm not surprised. Not really. It's what would look good to Thomas. He was always very concerned about appearances and doing what was socially acceptable. Us being buried all together, one tight-knit family, that's what he would make happen. Or at least make it appear to be true. In fact, it's only one third true. I'm reasonably certain that my husband lies in the United Church cemetery, and I'm sure that two others don't."

"Robert's in the flowerbed. So where are you?"

Katherine doesn't say anything, just turns away from me and looks back over the strait.

Eighteen

Here it is." I come to stand beside the gravestone, a perfect white ridge of snow along its top. On the ground itself, the snow forms a less even layer, our footprints black in the moonlight leading from the parking lot into the yard. Everything looks a bit different in the snow, but I watched for that bench and knew from that where to find the O'Leary stone.

In the end, this whole thing had been Mom's idea. Over endless cups of tea we talked and talked about a solution. Grammie suggested that maybe we call a priest and try to get Katherine exorcised from her house. This seemed like a harsh way to treat a friend.

Perhaps we should find the bodies of both Katherine and Baby Robert and have them buried in the cemetery. This was my idea. Mom shuddered, and Grammie said I couldn't pay her enough to do it.

"So what should we do then?" I asked, and both Grammie and I turned to look expectantly at Mom. She hadn't had much input into our discussion yet. In fact, while Grammie and I sat excitedly forward in our chairs, gripping our mugs and tossing ideas around,

Mom sat back in her seat, watching us closely, agreeing and disagreeing only as she needed to.

Otherwise, she looked thoughtful. Who knew she was already planning the entire event out in the privacy of her head?

"We'll have a memorial service for them both out at the cemetery."

Mom can be bossy, but some of her ideas are pretty good. This was one of those good ones.

"The moon's so bright tonight," I whisper. "I think I can see everything out here without the flashlight." Mom switches it off for a second, just until Grammie protests.

"Sylvia. Turn that on. I'm a blind old woman trying to make out where I am in a dark cemetery in the middle of the night." Grammie doesn't whisper and neither does Mom.

"Mom, it's ten o'clock, and when's the last time you made an eye appointment?" Mom sounds like she's scolding Grammie, but I hear that twinkle in her voice, like the kind you see in some people's eyes. I recognize it, but Grammie doesn't and tries to defend herself.

"It's…well…Dr. Rundell died, you know. He was a very good doctor, and I just don't feel comfortable about seeing anyone else."

"Didn't he die five years ago?"

Then I chime in, my left mitten beaded with the snow I've finished brushing from the headstone. "Yeah. I remember. We were here for summer holidays. Man, he was ancient!"

Mom reminds us exactly how ancient. "Ninety-two."

Grammie straightens up and brushes the bits of leaves and dirt from her gloves, annoyed. "All right, all right. I'll make an eye appointment."

"Tomorrow," Mom adds.

"Maybe tomorrow, maybe later. I don't know. When I get around to it." Grammie pulls off her gloves and puts her hands on her hips. "If you're so concerned about it, why don't you make one for me?"

Mom shrugs a half-shrug and smiles a little. "I will. Tomorrow."

Grammie forces out a sigh, and a shadow crosses her face as she realizes she just lost the battle. It's difficult to fight Mom and win. She's tricky. It was her idea to do this at night, to bring along a flashlight, to bring the candles.

I've been thinking about Katherine all night, the reasons for her doing what she did, the reason we're in the graveyard tonight arguing about dead optometrists. Now, wanting to justify her unreasonable actions, I blurt out, "Katherine was crazy, crazy with sadness. She loved that little baby more than anything—more than herself."

Mom looks hard at me for a long time. She doesn't say anything, and the look she's giving me is starting to creep me out.

"What?" I demand.

Mom tells me, "It's just that I understand how your ghost friend felt. It's exactly how I feel about you."

Then Grammie laughs too, adding, "And me about your mother." She reaches down with her free hand and ruffles Mom's hair as if she were a little girl. Mom shakes her hair out and smiles broadly now, a flash of white in the moonlight. She's beautiful. There's that weird tightness in my chest again and a lump in my throat. I swallow and my eyes feel wet.

I comment, "Yeah. We know."

Grammie laughs and Mom tells her, "She must've inherited her modesty from you, Mom."

It's starting to snow, big far-apart flakes. A huge snowflake lands on my nose. I don't brush it off, just let it melt on my skin and slide down my cheek like a tear. I smile to myself and stare out at the glowing landscape. In my head, I talk to Katherine, telling her, "I'll miss you, but I hope this works. More than anything, I'll miss you, and more than anything, I hope this works."

I'm carrying the two black metal candle holders. They're square-based and heavy, and each is about thirty centimetres tall. Patterns are cut into the metal— star and sun and moon shapes—so that the candles will cast these same shapes all over as they burn. I set these sturdy holders down by their handles, like pail handles, on either side of the O'Leary gravestone.

Grammie's got the wreath we made this afternoon all wrapped up in tissue paper and lying in a flat cardboard box. I love how it turned out and wish that Katherine could see it. The wreath, like the service, was Mom's idea. She took me shopping yesterday, Saturday, to a department store in Charlottetown.

"What kind of flowers should we put on this wreath, Charly?" Mom asked my opinion. She usually never asks my opinion.

I spotted the silk red roses in fat bunches. "I like

those." I touched one of the petals as Mom agreed. "Me too." She scooped up five bunches and put them in the blue basket along with the glue gun we'd selected one aisle over.

"Now what kind of background? We need some green stuff." I couldn't believe this! She was letting me choose the whole thing, like she trusted my taste or something. Or maybe she wanted it to be my special project. Either way, it was great of her. Really great.

"Hmmm..." We both scanned the huge selection of artificial leaves and branches that spread out before us in this fluorescent-lit garden of plastic, silk and nylon. Finally, my eyes stopped on something that didn't usually go with roses yet seemed to fit the occasion. "How about these?"

"Well...it's different but I think they could work." Mom rested her chin on her bent fingers as she thought for a minute. I watched her face as she studied the frost-tipped, long-needled pine branches. Finally, she looked at me with her face bright. It was almost as if I could see the finished product in her eyes. "Yes. They'll be perfect!"

At home in the afternoon, we spread our supplies out on the kitchen table and got to work. Grammie and I mostly watched and kept Mom's teacup topped up as her hands worked expertly to make the memorial wreath for Katherine and Baby Robert. After about half-an-hour, Grammie commented, "Sylvia, I had no idea you were so crafty!"

"Me, neither," I admitted. I guess I'm realizing that the

older I get, the less I know about my mom. Maybe she's someone I really don't know, even though I've been with her all my life. What a thought.

Grammie sets the box in the snow, and by the glow of the flashlight, she carefully unwraps the wreath. I'm surprised when she hands it to me. "Here, Charly. You do the honours. It's for your friend."

I take the wreath. "But Katherine was your friend, too."

Grammie smiles and squeezes my arm gently. "Yes. Was. She was my friend, but she's your friend *now*, and you're the one she's counting on."

The wreath turned out to be huge. I hang it over the left hand corner of the stone, where it won't obscure any of the writing carved below. Then I move the one candleholder out of the way, set it in front of the granite marker instead of beside. It looks good. Without saying anything, Grammie passes me the butane-powered candle lighter. It takes a couple of clicks to get a flame out. There is no breeze and those thick, white candles light easily. They cast a lot of light, but Mom leaves the flashlight turned on and holds before it the piece of paper she's just taken from her pocket.

As we'd discussed, Mom reads the prayer she's written, the first one she's ever written, and for her first one, it sure is good. She clears her throat, and Grammie and I bow our heads as she starts to speak, "Dear God, thank you for the lives of Katherine O'Leary and her baby Robert O'Leary. Thank you that both my mom and Charly could share in knowing Katherine. She has been a blessing to them both. Please let Katherine rest now. Amen."

"Amen." Grammie and I repeat the word softly and solemnly in the snow, and with my eyes closed tight, I think about how it feels good to pray. It kind of makes me feel not alone. Who knows? Maybe that's the point.

Grammie digs around in the deep, deep pocket of her winter coat to find her piece of paper, and Mom hands her the flashlight. I shuffle my feet as Grammie begins: "I was fortunate to know Katherine O'Leary when I was a little younger than Charly is now. She was a beautiful lady, kind, with a wonderful sense of humour. Katherine had a real zest for life and always enjoyed spending time with young people. I remember going to her house with a few friends to listen to records and eat cookies and visit. As a young girl, it felt to me that Katherine was the only adult who really understood me. It was as if she knew me, knew who I was. And I hope I've grown up to be a little like her, with her love of life and of people. I'd be so proud to think I was anything like her."

Grammie clears her throat and her tone changes. She's more sombre still when she continues to speak. "Now that Katherine is dead, I want her to be as at peace as she was when I first met her. I hope that we can help to accomplish this tonight." She waits a moment, and the space between us is filled up with silence. Then Grammie says, "Charly."

Now it's my turn. I wasn't going to write anything out, but both Grammie and Mom told me that writing it out would guarantee that I'd get to say exactly what I wanted to. That made sense. I take the flashlight, my fingers just beginning to feel the cold, and start to read.

"Katherine is one of the first people I met when I moved here." And suddenly she's there—standing in the moonlight next to a tree. She's wearing that elegant fur coat and her fancy zip-up boots. Her hair is down and over her shoulders, brushed out smooth and straight. She waves to me, and her lips are moving. She points to where Grammie's standing, I think, and makes a motion over her stomach. Katherine keeps motioning and talking, but I can't hear her. So I keep reading and hope that she can hear me. Then she stands still and seems to listen.

"It was so hard when I first moved here, and it's like Katherine was here just for me and just to help make it all easier. What a friend! Katherine did more than be real nice to me. That was great, and we had the best time! She showed me that adults can be so, so sad. Before I used to think that once we grew up, our problems would be gone. We wouldn't be scared or lonely or sad. Then I found out that everyone feels that way sometimes—and some people lots of the time." I look at Mom, and I see she's crying and that Grammie has put her arm around her daughter's shoulder. I stop reading and watch them while Katherine watches me from where she stands in the shadow of that tree. This time, she nods in the direction of Mom and Grammie, and smiles so wide that I can see her expression in the moonlight.

"Keep going, Charly," Grammie prompts me, sounding gentle yet insistent. I can tell by the way she says this that she likes what I've written. She hasn't seen Katherine yet, in her long coat and with her closed-lipped smile. Probably won't. Probably can't. I'm the lucky one here.

"I want to say thanks to Katherine for everything—for being my friend and for teaching me things. She's a friend and a teacher." I'm looking right at her now, and she's looking back, nodding as I talk, still smiling. "She was a terrific mom who did everything she could for her baby Robert. She really loved him and really looked after him. He died anyway, because babies sometimes do just die for no reason at all." When I say this, Katherine lifts her hand to her face and cradles her cheek in it as if it's hard now to hold her head up. She rocks her body from side to side slowly, concentrating and feeling. I hope she can hear me now, because I'm talking right to her.

"It's not your fault." And a baby boy, bundled up all warm, is suddenly there in her arms under that tree. I can see her surprise in the way her body moves to kind of catch Robert as he appears. Her face is shadowed now by the outstretched branches of the tree, so it's harder to see her expression, but I bet she's happy. More than happy.

"It's dark." Grammie says what I've been thinking. It *is* dark. That big shining moon and all those stars have disappeared behind the clouds, and the snowflakes are getting closer together. Grammie begins to hum what I instantly recognize as "Amazing Grace"—one of the few church songs I know. We didn't talk about doing this, but it sure seems right.

Mom joins in immediately, her voice strong and clear and carried through the air on snowflakes. I've never heard her sing like that. She sounds good. Me, I hum even when Grammie starts to sing as loud as Mom.

Amazing Grace, how sweet the sound,
That saved a wretch like me!
I once was lost but now I'm found,
Was blind but now I see.

Wretch. Now there's a word no one uses any more. Katherine's holding Robert tightly, close to her body, and seems to be watching us. I blink hard as a sudden gust of wind picks up the snow, obliterating Katherine and extinguishing the candles. When the snow settles and the wind dies, she's gone.

Nineteen

I'm scared. This is why I've put off doing this for two weeks now. If I get there and she's not gone, I won't know what to tell her. On the other hand, if it has worked and Katherine's found the courage to leave, I won't be happy, either. No matter what happens, I can't see any way that this isn't going to suck.

It seems like the snow that started at the graveyard the Sunday night we had the ceremony didn't stop until yesterday. There are two towering banks of it on either side of the road plowed up by the grader. Fresh caramel swirls of gravel and sand pattern the road's surface. Crews have been by with their trucks to keep this secondary road that leads out to Katherine's place from icing up. Since the snow has ceased and the sky has cleared, the temperature has dropped. This kind of weather reminds me of home, of Alberta. Cold and crisp.

My boots crunch the snow, and the mounds of it surrounding me muffle all other sounds. Just me and my footsteps on this route. Around the bend, the O'Leary house comes into view. Inside my heavy mitts, my palms are suddenly moist, but not from being too warm. Nothing could be too warm this November day, the air full of shards of ice, stabbing at my nose, at my cheeks. When I blink, my lashes leave traces of moisture beneath my eyes. I'm just glad there's no wind.

From a distance, Katherine's house looks like it has a fresh coat of shiny white paint. That's how thick the frost is on its walls and veranda, how bright the sun's glare. Mom and Grammie don't know I'm out here. They think I'm volunteering in the school library after class, shelving books with Nandini and Ashley, a couple of girls I've made friends with. If they knew, I think they'd want to come along, but I don't want them here. I want to be alone to do this. In case she's there, in case I have to break the news to Katherine. My friend.

After the plowed road, the snow surrounding the O'Leary house seems really deep. Actually, it *is* really deep—probably half a metre or more. Walking along the secondary route was much easier than trudging along off the main trail. I walk through the gate to avoid tripping over the wire buried beneath winter's white blanket and, as I do, nothing happens. No change in the seasons, in the house, in the yard. Everything stays the same, an old frosty house on an early November afternoon. My heart rises, then, just as suddenly, crashes. This is hard. So hard. I'd hope, if only I knew what to hope for. Instead, I breathe in deep and keep lifting my knees high, making my way toward the porch.

I struggle up the slope that indicates where the stairs leading up to the veranda are under all this snow. The first step I take, I stumble and fall forward into snow right up to my elbows. Bits of wet cold find their way into my mittens and melt instantly, wetting my hands and dribbling down to my fingertips. "Great. That's just great." I stand up, teeter a bit and keep on climbing.

I get to the top, take another deep breath and reach for the doorknob. Before I can grab it, though, the door swings open. "That's new," I comment out loud, then, leaning my head in though the doorway, I call out, "Katherine? Are you here?" I'm greeted by icy silence. I step over the threshold and try again, "Katherine?" I hear the whimper in my voice, the pleading. Still nothing.

I walk though the entry and down the hall, knowing now that she's not here but not wanting to believe it. Straining my eyes to pierce the gloom, I stare into the kitchen, clutching the wall for balance on my slippery, snowy boots. In the middle of that worn kitchen table, its paint chipped, its wood scarred, I spot a folded piece of paper. Next to the note sits Robert's teddy bear. Again, my heart thuds its hope. If this excitement keeps up, I'm gonna have a heart attack.

*   *   *

"You haven't read it yet?" Grammie asks me as I shake off my coat. I couldn't wait to get into the house to tell them both, so I blurted out my news as soon as I was in the door and handed the teddy bear to Grammie to hold.

"No." I'd snatched the paper, shoved it deep in my pocket and left. It's all crumpled now and damp in my hand.

Mom's standing there beside Grammie, holding the little plastic watering can she uses to water her plants. "How do you know it's from her if you haven't read it?" she wants to know.

I shrug. "I just do is all." I don't tell them about the door swinging open, welcoming me.

"Well, get in here then, girl," Grammie urges me, "and let's take a look at it."

My feet, out of their boots, tingle in my socks. My red fingertips feel the same way, stiff and full of pins and needles. Mom hasn't taken her eyes off me. Finally, she says what she's been thinking since I walked in and called out the news of my discovery. "You should've let me drive you. It's too far to walk in this weather, all the way out to the shore."

"Walk out where?" My sister appears in the archway dividing the kitchen from Grammie's living room. The three of us turn and look at her in a way that makes her ask suspiciously, "What?"

Grammie is the first to speak out of the startled silence. She doesn't try to cover up or anything. "Charly's found something over at the old O'Leary place. We're going to take a look at it."

"What is it?" Nikki takes a step into the living room.

Mom answers her. "We're not sure."

Grammie heads into the kitchen, brushing by Nikki and laying a hand on her shoulder as she does. "Anyone besides our frozen Charly need tea?" She doesn't wait for an answer. At the sink, she fills the kettle, pulls out four mugs and comes to join the rest of us at the table.

My feet are starting to ache, and my fingers tremble as I carefully unfold the paper. The first thing I notice is the date at the top: June 29th. She didn't put a year here, and I can picture her looking at an old calendar, glancing out the window at the weather and randomly choosing a day. The second thing I see is Katherine's signature at the bottom.

"Are you going to read it or not?" Nikki says.

So I begin.

Dearest Charly,

I'm so happy you found my letter. I knew you would. I can't think of where to start. It was so wonderful getting to know you. You're a great girl, and you remind me so much of your grammie, of Cosie. Your company made me feel alive again, and believe me, that's not easy!

Thank you to you and your mom and your grammie for the ceremony in the church cemetery. I was there, you know.

Let me get to the point. Your grammie is my daughter.

"What?" All four of us at the table say it at once. My hands start to shake, and I drop the letter to the tabletop.

"Whose daughter is Grammie?" Nikki wants to know all the details, and I don't think Grammie's able to give them to her. She stares at the partly-read letter on the table, and Nikki continues to look confused, but at least she shuts up. Mom reaches over, lays a hand on

Grammie's wrist, asks her, "Mom, did you know you were adopted?"

Grammie slowly turns her head toward Mom and says, "I wondered, but I didn't know for sure." She looks like our neighbour back in Alberta looked when he found his old dog dead in the alley behind his house. Someone had poisoned it. His face had crumpled up like a wet paper bag and stayed that way. Like Grammie's now. Mom grabs hold of Grammie's hand and pulls it under the table. A single tear, fat and shiny, slides down Grammie's wrinkled cheek. I don't know what to do, so I pick up the letter and keep on going.

The funny thing is that when I moved to the Island, it was to escape her memory. Dad and I both thought if I got away, married Thomas, I would feel better about things, about giving her up, that is. Then when I arrived here, there she was. I guess you can't always get away from your past. Thomas knew when I was young I'd had a child, but I never told him she lived in our town or who the father was. It's Gerald—remember? From the photo album?

I was so young when I had Cosie—only sixteen. In my imagination, I named her Elizabeth Cornelia. I begged the nurse to show me her before they took her away. She was beautiful! I cried for a year over the mistake I'd made.

After awhile, though, life got back to normal. I returned to school, caught up with my work, saw my friends again. Everyone was very nice. They treated me like I'd never been away, but of course they knew. Everyone knew. But nobody ever talked about it.

When Father met Thomas years later, he encouraged our courtship as much as he had discouraged marriage between Gerald and me. I was flattered by Thomas's attention and was hoping for another chance at marriage after the mistakes I'd made. I remember thinking that a new life would erase parts of my old life. As you know, I got my wish and became Mrs. Thomas O'Leary.

Be careful what you wish for, Charly. Tell your grammie to do the same. For a long time, I wished I were dead. Then I became pregnant with Robert, and my world changed. The idea of him made the world shine. Thomas was happy, too, when he was home, that is. He didn't spend a lot of time at home, but you know that. He wanted a boy, and that's what he got.

When Robert died, I died along with him. I did a shameful thing, Charly. I chose as my resting place the well out back of the house, and I want it to stay that way. Please.

There's a sharp gasp from Mom across the table, still clutching Grammie's hand.

"Chose her resting place? What's that s'posed to mean?" This from Nikki—of course.

I look up from the yellowed page I've been reading. "It means she killed herself." In my ears, my voice doesn't sound like my own. It's what I suspected, but I didn't want to know. Like when I was a little kid and was wondering about Santa Claus. Only this is worse. Way worse. I feel like there's a knife stuck in my throat.

"Oh." My sister doesn't say any more, and I read again.

I'm sorry, Charly. I don't mean for this to be all doom and gloom. There's some good news. Thomas collected gold coins, and the nature of his death meant that they were never found and claimed as part of the estate. There's a box of them under the floorboards of our cupboard in the bedroom. It would make me so happy if you'd take them.

Don't feel you have to if you don't want to, but it would make me even happier if you'd look after my house. I'm not there any more, but I still want you there. I hate the thought of it being empty, now that I'm gone. You seemed to fit in there. It's like you belonged.

Of course, this is a decision to be made within your family. Whatever you choose, you've got my blessing— for what it's worth!

I'm glad I had the chance to know you, my girl, my lovely great-granddaughter. Thank you from the bottom of my heart for all you've done for me. I'll miss you forever.

All my love,

Katherine

p.s. Please give the bear to Cosie. It was hers all along.

I can't feel the letter in my hands any more. My whole body's gone numb. I leave the letter lying on the table and stagger blindly up the stairs to my room. If

Mom or Grammie call out to my retreating back, I don't hear them. I close my bedroom door behind me and fall onto the bed. The last thing I see before I shut my eyes is that floppy sun hat Katherine gave me, hanging on the back of my desk chair.

Lori Knutson made her first visit to Prince Edward Island in 1994. A born and raised prairie girl, her imagination was sparked by the legends and history of the Island, especially those stories surrounding West Point and the Northumberland Strait.

Lori has worked as a beekeeper, an interpreter at an historical village, a United Church lay preacher and a bookseller. She currently works as an elementary school teacher. Her first book, a devotional called *Sacred Simplicities,* was published in 2004.

Lori lives in Hughenden, Alberta.

She can be visited on the web at loriknutson.com